a good horse

a good horse

Jane
Smiley

with illustrations by Elaine Clayton

ALFRED A. KNOPF
NEW YORK

THIS IS A BORZOI BOOK PUBLISHED BY ALFRED A. KNOPF

This is a work of fiction. Names, characters, places, and incidents either are the product of the author's imagination or are used fictitiously. Any resemblance to actual persons, living or dead, events, or locales is entirely coincidental.

Text copyright © 2010 by Jane Smiley
Illustrations copyright © 2010 by Elaine Clayton

All rights reserved. Published in the United States by Alfred A. Knopf, an imprint of Random House Children's Books, a division of Random House, Inc., New York.

Knopf, Borzoi Books, and the colophon are registered trademarks of Random House, Inc.

Visit us on the Web! www.randomhouse.com/kids

Educators and librarians, for a variety of teaching tools, visit us at
www.randomhouse.com/teachers

Library of Congress Cataloging-in-Publication Data
Smiley, Jane.
A good horse / Jane Smiley ; with illustrations by Elaine Clayton. — 1st ed.
p. cm.
Summary: On her family's California horse ranch in the 1960s, eighth-grader Abby Lovitt faces the possibility of giving up her beloved colt, Jack, when it comes to light that his dam might have been stolen.
ISBN 978-0-375-86229-8 (trade) — ISBN 978-0-375-96228-8 (lib. bdg.) —
ISBN 978-0-375-89415-2 (e-book)
[1. Horses—Training—Fiction. 2. Ranch life—California—Fiction. 3. Family life—California—Fiction. 4. Christian life—Fiction. 5. Swindlers and swindling—Fiction. 6. California—History—1950—Fiction.] I. Clayton, Elaine, ill. II. Title.
PZ7.S6413Goo 2010
[Fic]—dc22
2009051264

The text of this book is set in 11.5-point Goudy.

Printed in the United States of America
October 2010
10 9 8 7 6 5 4 3 2
First Edition

Random House Children's Books supports the First Amendment and celebrates the right to read.

a good horse

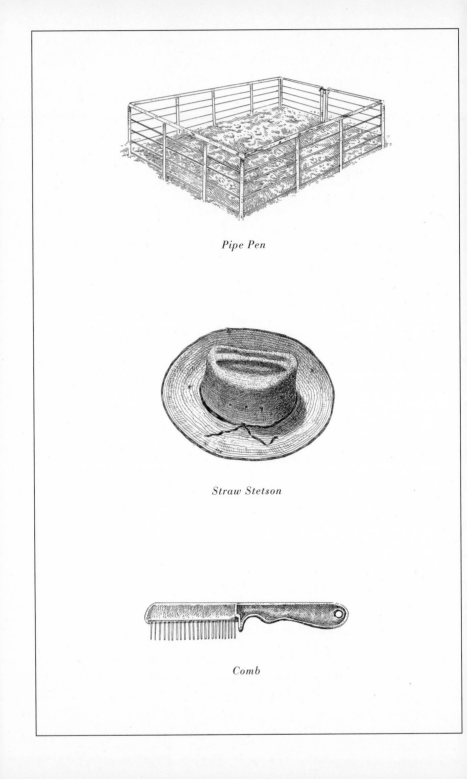

Pipe Pen

Straw Stetson

Comb

Chapter 1

THE LETTER ARRIVED ON MY BIRTHDAY. ALL THROUGH ELEMENtary school, I was kind of mad that my birthday came so early in the year, September 13, because people at school—teachers, students, the ladies in the lunchroom, even the moms—weren't yet thinking about cupcakes in class or singing "Happy Birthday" at lunch. As the school year progressed, every birthday got to be a bigger and bigger deal, and by March (when the Goldman twins had their birthday), there were party hats and little favors and a big "Happy Birthday" on the blackboard in colored chalk. On September 13, though, school was too new; no one was tired of it yet, so if Mom sent cookies, sometimes the teacher would forget to hand them out until the end of the day, and then the kids grabbed them, and took them on the school bus, and forgot why they were there. It kind of made me mad and it kind of made me sad.

But in junior high, birthdays at school were a thing of the past for everybody. Even so, Gloria and Stella each brought me something: Stella gave me a small stuffed unicorn, and Gloria brought me a book called *C. W. Anderson's Complete Book of Horses and Horsemanship*. This was a big, expensive book, and I guessed that Gloria's mom had picked it out. No cookies. But the whole setup was different in eighth grade—we went to different classrooms, and not everyone was in all the same classes together. I had English, algebra, and biology with Gloria, and Stella was in our algebra class, and Stella and I had French and social studies. We all had phys ed at the same time, at least until it got cold and we either passed our required swimming tests or gave up on them. After that, Stella said she was going to play basketball—she had been practicing her jump shot all summer.

The Big Four had been split up and got mixed around—we didn't even call them the Big Four anymore. It was almost funny to think how they had run the whole seventh grade, and now, three months later, no one paid much attention to them. And so school was dull. It was all business: *"J'ai une soeur et un frère. Mon frère s'appelle Jean et ma soeur s'appelle Annette"*; "If A is greater than B, and C is greater than D, and D is less than A, then what is the value of B?" "Christopher Columbus was not the first European to discover the western hemisphere. That honor goes to Leif Eriksson, who was a Viking from Iceland, the son of Erik the Red, who discovered Greenland"; and "Even though it looks red, blood consists of red blood cells and white blood cells. These two types of cells have very different functions." In eighth grade, it was important to take good notes. I had five different notebooks for my classes. (The fifth was for home economics—"All foods are made up of proteins, fats, and starches." The boys took shop.)

And so school was about the same every day, which I didn't mind, because there was a lot going on at home, with Black George and Jack and the horses Daddy had gotten through Uncle Luke over the summer, that I needed a rest at school, not the sort of rest where you lie down and sleep but the sort of rest where you know what is going to happen every minute even if it isn't much fun.

I saw the letter when I got off the school bus and took the mail out of the mailbox by the road. It was right on top. What caught my eye was not the address: "Mr. Mark Lovitt, Oak Valley Ranch," et cetera, but the return address: "Brandt and Carson Agency, 3802 Lovers' Lane Circle, Dallas, Texas." I thought that was such a funny address. And the envelope was nice, too, not like a bill. But I didn't think about it again once I got in the house, because right there, at the kitchen table, was Jem Jarrow, drinking a glass of water and smiling, and Mom was sitting across from him, grinning and saying, "Abby! Happy birthday, sweetheart!"

So I threw down my books and the letters and ran upstairs to put on my jeans and boots, and the three of us went out to find Jack. This was my birthday present! A training session with Jem Jarrow! I hadn't seen him in months, and it was the best birthday present I could have thought of.

Jem was smaller than I remembered, walking in front of

me, in those boots that looked like they had molded themselves around his feet, with his pale straw Stetson pushed back on his head. But no, probably not. It was me who was bigger—I knew I had grown at least two inches since the spring. I was almost as tall as Mom. What Daddy said about this was "Once your feet stop growing, then you top out," which always made Mom laugh, but it was a good question.

Mom had topped out at five foot three, size-six shoes, but Daddy hadn't topped out until six feet, size ten, same with my brother Danny. And somewhere back there in Oklahoma, where my grandparents and relatives still lived, was Aunt (or Great-aunt) Alice, who had topped out at five-eleven back when most women didn't see five-two. "You never know when that might crop up again" was what Daddy said the last time he'd bought me a pair of boots, size seven (but a little too big so they would last through the winter), and even though he was smiling, well, you never did know, did you?

Jem was the sort of horse trainer who didn't expect to come back and tell you the same things over and over—he expected you to learn from him how horses' minds worked and then to build on what you'd learned. In the spring, he'd helped me with a very grumpy horse that I was rather afraid of. My birthday surprise was that we went to the barn rather than to the gelding corral. Right there in the barn beside the chocolate cake on a card table was Daddy holding my eight-month-old colt, Jack. Jack had a red ribbon with a blue bow looped around his neck, and some more ribbons braided into his forelock, and when he saw me, he whinnied and pricked his ears. And even though I had fed him before going to school that

4

morning and I saw him every single day and he always trotted over to the fence as soon as I approached and stretched his head out for a pat, and then followed me to the gate, and was in every way a kind and affectionate horse, there was something about this whinny and the way he tossed his head to say "Hey! You're home! I missed you! Let's do something!" that brought tears to my eyes because I was so lucky. So I went up to Daddy and took the lead rope out of his hand and led Jack out of the barn, and he turned in a curve around me and then put his head down so I would pat him along the neck, and then he gave a low nicker, just for me.

Jem Jarrow was smiling. He said, "Let's see what this fellow has learned." In addition to helping me with Ornery George (who was now sold), Jem had shown me how to give Jack his first lessons in being a good boy.

I led him toward what had once been his pen. It was now the training corral, dusty and tan-colored, because Daddy had brought in a load of sand and the three of us had raked it into the dirt. He had plans for the winter, some way he was going to work the footing so it would drain perfectly after every rainstorm, but there hadn't been any rain since April, and there probably wouldn't be any until December, so it was no rush.

The hills that spread up and away were the purest gold this time of year, creased here and there by streambeds and dotted with oaks, rising to the hard, endless, cloudless blue of the sky. Over to the east, around the crown of Rory's Peak, some of Mr. Jordan's cattle lay under the trees, not stretched out like they were sleeping but heads up and thoughtful, chewing their cud. Mr. Jordan had a huge ranch, and he only put cows in this field around this time of year, to save the grass from getting eaten down to the roots. The cows were beautiful, I thought, a special breed of blue Brahmas, with long ears and quiet expressions. They didn't mind the heat, according to Daddy, not like Angus and even Herefords, who had been bred for cool weather. And they were really blue. Once in a while, I liked to ride one of the horses up the hill to the fence line, then get off and pet them through the wire. It was good for the horses to go up and down the hill, and also to get used to the cows, at least a little.

I opened the gate and walked through, making sure that Jack was right with me, neither lagging behind (but he never did that) nor pulling me forward. He was good. He stepped through, and when I twitched the rope, he swung around and dropped his head. I unbuckled the halter. He waited until I waved him off, and then, having been given permission, he trotted away, tail up, ears pricked, neck arched. The four mares in the mares' corral looked up from their hay as if he was something to watch.

And he was.

Whatever there had been of the baby in Jack was gone now. His rough foal coat had shed out, leaving smooth, rich silk the color of dark chocolate, which shaded into mahogany around his nose and on his belly just in front of his stifle. The black of his legs ran above the knees, and his tail had started to grow out—it was no longer fluffy and brown but was beginning to be smooth and black. His mane was still sticking up, thin and soft, but his forelock had begun to grow—it even had a cowlick, right in the center, and every day when I brushed him, I liked to smooth it together between my fingers. It would hold together for maybe a second, and then the two halves would spring apart again, one half falling toward his left eye and one half falling toward his right eye.

His eyes were big and black, "eyes you could knock off with a stick," Daddy said, but he didn't mean that in a bad way—he meant that Jack's eyes were prominent and bright, always looking and always taking things in. Even at eight months old, Jack was quite a sight, or at least I thought so—long-legged still, but muscular and strong, and big. He trotted across the pen and then swept around and sped up and then crossed in front of me, his neck arched. Then he sprang off his hind legs. Everyone was quiet until Daddy said in his usual way, "Useless animal, if you ask me," but he said it in a voice that showed that usefulness wasn't everything—sheer gorgeousness was worth something, too. Maybe.

Jem Jarrow said, "Usefulness is in the eye of the beholder, I think." He went into the center of the pen with his rope coiled in his right hand and stood there in his normal way, not doing anything, just watching the horse.

Then Jack realized that he was free. The first thing he did was rear up, with a little squeal, and stretch his forelegs upward. He stayed like that for what seemed like a long time, and then dropped and galloped across the pen, kicking up and squealing. In the other corner, he turned suddenly toward Jem and reared again, this time looking right at him—not stretching his forelegs out but curling them in, as if to say, Look at me! Look what I can do! But I would never hurt you!

He stood up like that, once again, for a long moment, and then actually took a step on his hind legs like a circus horse, and Jem Jarrow laughed. Jack came down and trotted across the pen in front of us, snorting and full of himself. Then Jem lifted the coil of rope and turned his body. Jack went right to his circle at a fast trot. Jem kept the coil lifted, and Jack flicked his ear toward it, knowing that that meant for him to keep going. After four circuits, Jem lowered the coil and Jack slowed down. When Jem stepped back, Jack stepped under and spun inward, then headed in the other direction. Jem hardly had to lift his rope at all—Jack just kept trotting, arching his neck and sometimes tossing his head. It was a beautiful sight. I felt myself getting mesmerized. And then Jem called out, "He's quick, all right, and proud. But you've done a good job, Miss Abby. He's ready as can be for the next step."

That was the best birthday present ever.

I said, "What's the next step?"

Jem motioned to me to come to the middle of the pen. When I got there, we stood quietly. After a minute or two, Jack, who had been walking along the side of the pen, turned and walked toward us, his ears pricked. Jem stood quietly, the coil down. When Jack stopped in front of us, looking at us, Jem slipped the coil over his neck. Then we stood there for another few moments. Jack's ears flicked back and forth. Jem slowly, and in a relaxed way, took a few steps along Jack's left side, and then went around behind him, bringing the rope across below his tail, then he took a step and another step along his right side.

Jack was now wrapped in the rope. Jem exerted just a little pressure, Jack flicked his ears and then turned away from Jem and unwound himself. It seemed like no big deal. It seemed like the natural thing to do. But it wasn't. Lots of horses wouldn't think to unwind themselves; they would panic and pull back or try to pull their legs out and maybe get tangled up. Unwinding himself was just what you wanted a horse to do. Jem did this again to the left, and then twice to the right, and then he had me hold the rope and do the winding. By the time I was done with two turns in each direction, Jack was hardly letting himself be wound—as soon as he felt the least pressure from the rope, he simply followed it, looking at me and waiting for the next thing.

The next thing was important, too. I left the pen, and Jem lassoed Jack's forefoot. You can say he lassoed it, but really, he more or less offered a loop, Jack stepped into it, and Jem tightened the loop. Jack startled and then lifted his foot, but then he put it down. They stood there for a moment. Jem loosened the rope, and Jack stepped out of it. After that, Jem did the same thing with each foot. When he was doing the back feet, Jack was more worried—he kicked out and tried to jump away, but finally, he stood quietly. Mom said, "What's he doing this for?"

Daddy said, "My guess, he wants the horse to learn to stop and stand still if it gets caught in something. Good idea, too. My cousin Cal had a mare who got caught in a loose strand of barbed wire when we were kids. By the time we found her, she'd cut herself to the bone trying to get free. Had to put her down. Cal cried for days."

We all shook our heads.

I said, "We ought to teach all of them this."

Daddy said, "We ought to."

But it was the sort of "We ought to" that he said when I said, "Let's go to Hawaii," or "Let's make the training pen round." He meant it, but he also meant, Who has time for that? And in fact, who did? Including Jack and Black George, we had nine horses, which was a lot. We were both riding four horses every day, and even Mom was riding—Lincoln and Jefferson, two quiet horses who were good on the trail. Mom got on them each three times a week and rode them around the ranch at a walk. Daddy was going to sell them to someone as trail horses—maybe one of the resorts over by the coast. Daddy would say, "It's okay if you fall off—they have to learn to stop and stand there if you do."

Mom said, "Thanks, but no thanks."

Jem called me into the arena. He had put Jack's halter on him again, the one with the long lead rope, and he showed me how to use that rope to give Jack a little winding and unwinding practice. He said, "Not all the time. But once in a while. We don't want to work him like a two-year-old—he's just a baby. But the sooner he learns a few things, the more they get to be second nature to him."

"Like keeping quiet when he's caught in something."

"Just like that."

Then he showed me how to snake the end of the rope around his ankles and forelegs, just quickly, just to get him used to it, so he wouldn't flinch and wouldn't try to get away. I did it a few times. Jack was alert, but he didn't move. Jem said, "You got a rope of your own?"

"No."

"Well, practice a little with your Daddy's rope, and we can

try this sometime. I worked with a horse on the ranch a couple of years ago, just like this. 'Bout six months later, I had that fella in a pipe pen with some other horses. I fed the three of them and then went off to do some other work. When I came back an hour later, that one was lying down flat on his side, and he had his front ankle wedged under the pipe pen. He was just lying there. And he just lay there quietly until I managed to get his foot out of there, which took me ten minutes, anyway. Horse who's caught has got to let himself be caught and be patient about it. It's not second nature for them."

The whole time, we were snaking the rope around under Jack's feet, and he was standing there like it was nothing, just staring at Jem and then at me. Jem stopped and patted Jack in a long stroke down his neck. I couldn't help myself, I kissed him on the nose.

Jem took a piece of chocolate cake away with him, and then, after he was gone, since it was still light and a nice day, I got on Black George and Daddy got on his favorite, one I had named Lester. We took them to the arena while Mom went in the house to cook something mysterious that was probably fried chicken, since that was my favorite.

Lester was a buckskin, really golden with a black mane and tail, about five years old, and a horse Daddy might have kept for himself if Daddy did that sort of thing, which I had never seen him do. Daddy had gotten Lester from a man up by Hollister, who was leaving town very suddenly and wasn't saying why. Daddy guessed that he owed a lot of money to someone and he didn't want Lester to have to be part of that payment. Daddy and Mom talked about this for a couple of nights—I could hear them from my room, since the windows were open—and Mom didn't like it, but Daddy said that the man had just gotten in over his head and however we felt about him walking away from his debts, it was not right for a good horse like Lester to have to pay the price, since once the bank got ahold of him, there was no telling where he would end up. So we got Lester. He had been with us for about three months, and I knew Daddy would sell him, but only, as he said, "If the right party comes along."

Black George, in the meantime, was as good as gold and had been all summer, and we had him entered in the October show over on the coast. I was to ride in two classes, and Miss Slater was to help us with Black George for three classes "gratis," which meant "for free." Daddy said that "gratis" was all very well, but when she saw Black George jump, she would be quick as a bunny finding him a new owner, and she would get her commission, which was worth gratis any day.

I hadn't seen Miss Slater, who taught English-style riding out at a big, fancy barn on the coast, for months, though we talked once in a while on the phone about the pony we'd sold to her client, which she named Gallant Man after a famous racehorse. The girl we'd sold the pony to, Melinda, had spent the summer down south, wherever they lived, maybe it was Hollywood, or maybe it was Brentwood—one of the woods— and then stayed there to go to school "because of the divorce." I can't say that I missed Melinda, but I can't say that I didn't, either. I *thought* about her and *wondered* about her. Missing someone is more about wanting to be with them. I missed Danny.

Black George wasn't terribly black anymore—he had been standing out in the sunshine all summer, so across his back he was a little faded and red. But other than that, he was fine-looking and in excellent condition—all summer long, two days a week, I had ridden him up and down hills for at least an hour. It had been a little scary at first, because he was young and didn't know how to go down a hill with a rider on him. He had to learn to bend his hocks and stifles and relax his back while keeping his head and neck balanced. I had to remember to ask him to do these things by sitting up straight with my heels down and my shoulders and head relaxed but square and my seat deep in the saddle. It was a little like sledding down a big hill in one of those saucer sleds—you sat deep and felt the horse going down just a little in front of you.

It was good for his muscles to go up hills—for that, you leaned forward and let him put his head down and climb, except that after a few weeks, Black George got pretty strong and made it clear to me that he wanted to trot or canter up, and I let him. It was fun. At any rate, as a result of this plus our other work, and also because he lived outside and ran around with the other geldings, he was muscular and fit. Daddy expected to get a lot of money for him, maybe five or six thousand dollars.

The show we were taking him to was the key. Daddy had picked out a set of classes in the local hunter division. The fences would be three feet. Three feet was easy as pie for Black George, and only about three inches taller than the fences I had jumped with the pony, while Black George was eight inches taller than the pony and had much longer legs. We had jumped all sorts of things over the summer, and Black George had liked it—the stacked hay bales, the kitchen chairs set in a row, a length of picket fence, a length of picket fence with a tablecloth hanging over it, a row of Mom's potted geraniums (which were pretty tall) sitting on a bench, the bench itself with another bench on top of it. About the only thing we hadn't jumped was regular poles between two standards, the very thing that you were supposed to jump at a horse show. But Daddy and Miss Slater had made a plan, and we were to go over to the stable a week before the show and try some of those.

Now we walked, trotted, and cantered Lester and Black George around the arena, and I was reminded of lessons I had taken on Black George with Jem Jarrow. I made myself not be lazy and remember what it felt like to make him bend to the inside and balance himself around the turns, what it felt like to ask him to step under, what it felt like when he lifted his front end and relaxed his back. What it felt like was heaven. The really interesting part was that after he got used to it again (I had been lazy for what seemed like months), he was happier, too, and went along full of energy and quiet all at the same time.

Earlier in the day, Daddy had ridden Happy, a new one he thought he could sell as a cow horse, so all we were left with were Sprinkles and Sunshine. We rode them until almost dark. Daddy had someone coming to look at Sprinkles over the weekend. Her best thing was her trot—she could trot all day and it was comfortable and smooth. "She would have made a great mailman's horse," he said, "back in the old days when they delivered mail on horseback. But there's always a use for a horse that can cover ground." Sunshine hadn't discovered her talents yet. I was beginning to think maybe she didn't have anything special, but she was a kind, friendly horse and I liked her.

When we went in for dinner, I saw that it was fried chicken and twice-baked potatoes, and there was a card at my plate from Danny, and Daddy didn't say a word about it, even about the ten-dollar bill that fell out of the envelope. That was a letter in the mail that I hadn't noticed.

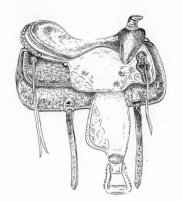

Western Saddle

English Stirrups

English Saddle

Chapter 2

It was the next night, after dinner, that Daddy showed me the letter from Lovers' Lane Circle. It read:

Dear Mr. Lovitt,

My name is Howard W. Brandt. I am a private investigator with the Brandt and Carson Agency, in Dallas, Texas. We have been engaged to look into the circumstances surrounding the transfer of ownership of a horse, to you, from a Mr. Robert Hogarth, of By Golly Horse Sales of Lawton, Oklahoma. It is our understanding that you purchased four horses from Mr. Hogarth on November 12 of last year and that you transported these animals to your home in California. It is our belief that one of these animals may have been a dark bay mare, aged nine, named Alabama Lady, who was in foal to a stallion belonging to Mr. Warner Wilson Matthews III. Alabama Lady disappeared from Mr. Matthews's property, Wheatsheaf Ranch, on or about October 1 of last year, along with three other mares. Please let us know by return mail if you purchased a mare who produced a foal early this year.

Unfortunately, the mare has no white markings. She is about sixteen hands tall, of medium build. She has a cowlick on either side of her neck, about four inches back from her ears, and she also has a cowlick in her forelock, which prevents her forelock from falling smoothly forward. She has no other distinguishing marks. She was tattooed on the underside of her upper lip at the racetrack as a two-year-old, but this tattoo may have faded or be unreadable. Mr. Matthews is most interested in tracing this mare, as she is well bred and has produced excellent foals. There is a reward for her return.

Thank you for your attention.

Yours truly,
Howard W. Brandt

All I could say after I read this letter was "I guess we figured he's a Thoroughbred, huh?"

"And a good one," said Daddy.

At first, that was all I thought about it—that now we knew that Jack was a real Thoroughbred, with a pedigree as long as your arm. I went out before bed and walked over to the gelding corral. Jack was standing beside Black George, and both had their heads down. Lester was stretched out on his side a little ways out in the pasture, and Lincoln and Jefferson were snuffling around for bits of hay or grass. I didn't call or say anything—sometimes it's more fun to watch the horses do what they want to, even when they don't want to do much. Just then, Black George lay down, giving a long groan, as if he was too tired to stand on his feet anymore. Jack looked at him for a moment, then gave him a push with his nose. Black George didn't respond, so Jack tossed his head and trotted over to Lincoln and Jefferson. They each pinned their ears a little bit, to remind him who the grown-ups were, but then Lincoln, who was a little younger than Jefferson, squealed and kicked up. Then he and Jack galloped for a few strides. Right then I could see that Jack was the Thoroughbred—he kept up perfectly with Lincoln and had more energy. When Lincoln dropped to a trot after half a dozen strides, Jack kept on going to the pasture fence and then trotted back. His ears were pricked and he was ready to play.

I whistled and he turned toward me, all alert now. When he saw me, he trotted straight over. I petted him on the head and around the eyes, and I smoothed his forelock. So that's where he got it. I whispered, "Alabama Lady. That's a nice name." We, of course, had called her Jewel, like all of the other mares. Brown Jewel, which wasn't much of a name at all. You couldn't even think of a precious stone, like a sapphire or a ruby, that was a brown jewel. For a while after Jack was born, I called her Pearl in my own mind, but I didn't say it out loud, and it made me sad that we hadn't named her something prettier than Brown Jewel.

It was only in the middle of the night, after I woke up from a dream about Danny calling Mom and telling her he had driven his car all the way to France (*"Paris est une grande ville en France. À Paris, les Parisiens fait beaucoup des choses agréables!"* or something like that), that I realized that there was more to the discovery of Jack's mom than I had been thinking about. I had spent so much time with him from the day he was born, and had thought about him so much, and loved him so much, that it hadn't occurred to me he wasn't my horse. But maybe, in actual fact, he wasn't.

After that, I didn't go to sleep for a long time, and when I did get up. I was so tired feeding the horses that I slept on the school bus in spite of the fact that two of the seventh-grade boys were throwing a Wiffle ball back and forth over my head from the front of the bus all the way to the rear, and the bus driver pulled over to take the ball away from them, at which point, one of the boys threw it out the open window. That I could have this kind of fuss going on all around me and still doze off showed just how tired I was.

All through English and biology, Gloria was staring at me, and she even had to poke me at one point and say, "Wake up, *she's* looking at you!" At lunch, before Stella sat down (she was talking to Linda A.), Gloria said, "So what's wrong with you? You look like they pulled you feetfirst through a privet hedge." Gloria loved this saying. It must have been one her dad used. I had no idea what it meant, really, but I always gave her a smile when she said it. This time, I told her, "I might have to give up Jack."

"You're kidding! Doesn't your dad realize yet that that would kill you?"

"It's not—"

"Well, I don't mean literally kill you."

"I know. But what's the difference? Anyway, Daddy has nothing to do with it. Remember the mare, Brown Jewel, his mom—I mean, his dam?"

"Yes. She died."

"Well, this guy wrote and said that she belonged to someone and somehow got away, and maybe the guy who sold her to us shouldn't have."

"But the mom died."

"Daddy's going to tell this guy that. He's a private investigator."

It was at this point that I realized that the person behind me was listening to us. I bent down and whispered, "From Texas. He's a private detective from Texas."

"Well, your dad paid the money. It's not his fault whatever happened to the mare. Didn't you say that she was kind of a mess when you got her?"

"She was thin, and her feet were all cracked and broken."

"Well, if you got a horse who was a mess, and you saved her, then it isn't fair—"

Now the person behind me cleared his throat, and I turned around and saw that it was Brian Connelly. I hadn't realized that he was sitting there. He sniffed and said, "That's accepting stolen goods."

"Excuse me?" said Gloria.

"If you buy something that's been stolen, that's accepting stolen goods. You can go to jail for that. I saw about that on *The F.B.I.*"

Gloria said, "Do you learn everything you know from television, Brian?" Then she turned her back to him and pushed me down the bench, saying, "Don't listen to him. He doesn't know what he's talking about."

I glanced back at Brian. It was true, he didn't always know, or often know, what he was talking about, but maybe this time he did. Now Stella came over, sat down, and opened her lunch bag. She pulled out an apple and an orange. She said, "This morning, I saw I lost four pounds. That's since Sunday."

Gloria looked into Stella's bag. She said, "That's all you're having for lunch?"

"I'm not hungry. I don't know if I will be able to eat this much."

Well, it was a big orange. Gloria said, "Listen to this," but then I caught her eye and shook my head. She pursed her lips and gave me a little nod. Stella said, "I have a small frame, so I should weigh no more than 108. I'll be there in a week at this rate."

Gloria said, "I could never eat just an apple and an orange for lunch. Never in a million years." She took a bite out of her peanut butter sandwich.

That night after dinner, Daddy showed me the letter he had written to Mr. Brandt. It read:

Dear Mr. Brandt,

Thank you for your letter. Among the horses I purchased from By Golly Horse Sales in November, there was a brown mare. I paid $650 for her. She was in poor condition, and I was told by the manager of By Golly Horse Sales that she had been there less than ten days. I could see that she was a nice horse, though. She did foal out a colt in the middle of January, but I am sorry to say that she died about a month later, probably of colic. I was away from my ranch at the time.

Yours truly,
Mark Lovitt
Oak Valley Ranch

Mom was sitting across the kitchen table when he handed me this letter, and then they both sat there while I read it, and then they both looked at me when I was finished, so I knew that we were having a talk. I pushed the letter to the center of the table.

Daddy said, "You never know what the Lord will bring us, Abby."

"The Lord giveth and the Lord taketh away." I said this so that he wouldn't have to.

"He isn't necessarily going to take anything away" was what Mom said, then I heard Daddy draw his breath in through his nose the way he did when he was trying to be careful.

He said, "To be honest with you, Abby, I don't know any more about this than these two letters. Brown Jewel was a brown mare. She had no markings, and I don't remember her cowlicks, if I ever looked at them. Sixteen-hand brown mares are about as unremarkable as a horse could be. Bobby Hogarth wasn't even there for those weeks, because he was in the hospital with pneumonia, and it didn't strike me that the fellow who was running the place had much sense, so I'm not jumping to conclusions about who Brown Jewel was or where she came from. I suggest that you put this letter out of your mind."

I nodded.

Mom said, "Brown Jewel was Brown Jewel. Don't make her into this mare until we know more, okay?"

I nodded again. I didn't say a thing about Jack's cowlick.

I went upstairs and did my homework, then I took a bath and went to bed. As I was lying there, I could hear the front door slam through my open window, and I knew that Daddy was going out to check the horses one last time. I realized, of course, that I could pray. We prayed for all sorts of things. But there were rules about praying, and one of them was that you could not petition the Lord. You could not decide what you wanted and then pray for that. You always had to pray for the right thing to happen, and, as anyone could tell you, the right thing to happen wasn't always the thing you wished for. Personally, I always wondered if breaking this rule about petitioning the Lord meant that you were less likely to get whatever it was you wanted than you would have been if you hadn't petitioned the Lord. Rules were rules, as everyone knew, and breaking them was a risky business.

On the other hand, if I prayed for the right thing to happen, I thought, wasn't that being dishonest? If someone was going to come and take Jack away from us, I wasn't sure I would want that even if it were the right thing. So, I didn't pray. And if the Lord was my personal savior, then he would know what was going on, anyway, without me telling him. I sat up and looked out the window toward the gelding pasture, even though

I couldn't see it from my corner of the house. I looked toward it and listened for the low sounds of the horses. But I thought no thoughts and said no prayers. That seemed to be the safest thing to do.

My birthday present was Jem Jarrow coming for two sessions, and the second session was Saturday morning. The weather was so warm those days that Mom was tending to the windows all day long—shades down, shades up, windows open, windows closed, fan on, fan off, all depending on whether it was warming up outside or cooling off, and whether the outside temperature was cooler or warmer than the inside temperature. As for the horses, we had one trail that ran down along the crick, in the shade of some trees, and there were a few places where the crick still had water in it, though only about six inches. We would ride the trail and stand in the water and call it a day. But when Jem Jarrow showed up, I forgot about the heat. Jack didn't seem to care and neither did Jem Jarrow—he was dressed in his same clothes, and his sleeves weren't even rolled up.

We took Jack to the pen, which at least was on the west side of the barn and a little in the shade. I took off the halter. Jack trotted around me, tossing his head, then stopped at the gate and gave Jem a sniff or two. Jem stood quietly, as usual, and let Jack smell his hands and his shirt, then he stroked his neck and gently waved him off. Jack came toward me, but then something caught his eye and he snorted and kicked out. I went out of the pen and Jem came in. He had his coil of rope. For a few minutes, he encouraged Jack in his running around. Bit by bit, Jack started paying attention to him, and pretty soon he was trotting his best trot, slightly curved away from Jem, his head and neck and back and even his tail loose and relaxed. Jem let him do this for a while, then turned his body so that Jack came into the center.

Jem uncoiled his rope and laid the loop—a fairly small loop—on the ground. After a moment, Jack stepped his left foot into it, and Jem tightened the rope around his ankle. Jack tried to pull his foot away, but only for a second. Almost immediately, he seemed to remember the lesson from three days before. He put his hoof down flat on the ground and looked at Jem. Jem tightened the rope a little. After a moment of thought, Jack picked up his foot and set it down again, a little closer to Jem. Jem loosened the rope and gave Jack a quick pat on the neck. Then he tightened the rope again. This time, Jack picked up his foot right away and held it up until Jem pulled it with the rope. It was almost as if he were guiding Jack to put his foot down in exactly the right place. I said, "Why are you doing that?"

He did it one more time—tension on the rope, foot comes up, tension on the rope, foot sets down a step ahead. Of course, the other feet were following along, but Jack and Jem were only paying attention to the foot with the rope around the ankle.

Jem said, "Well, for one thing, if he gets something wrapped around his foot—say, out in the pasture—that thing isn't always going to stay in one place. There are lots of ways for a horse to get caught or stuck. Sometimes, he needs to react by going along, not just by standing still. But in addition to that, this is another thing I'm asking him to do. I'm asking him to come along with me. It's the same as a halter or a rope around his neck, but it's around his foot. That's worth knowing."

"You mean, no matter what, when you want him to come along with you, he's got to come along with you."

"That's right, Miss Abby," said Jem.

They worked at this for another few minutes. Jack got used to it. He stopped looking down at his foot, and his ears stopped flicking back and forth, and pretty soon, as soon as he felt the pull of the rope, he stepped forward until Jem turned toward him and in that way told him not to.

After the left front came the right front. A horse, my daddy says, has two brains, a left brain and a right brain, and the two aren't always as connected as they could be. Sometimes, the horse will know something perfectly well on the right and then not know the same thing at all on the left, like taking the left lead at the canter or taking the right lead. Daddy always said that a horse being right-handed or left-handed came from how they lay inside the mare before they were born. I don't know if that is true. But at any rate, you had to teach the right side and then you had to teach the left side, and vice versa, in order for both sides of the brain, and both sides of the body, to develop equally.

Just a few days earlier, maybe a day or two before my birthday, I had said this very thing to Kyle Gonzalez, because Kyle was writing out our English sentences in study hall with his left hand. I happened to know from when we did our mission project that Kyle was right-handed, but when I asked him about it, he said he was developing the right side of his brain, and so he was writing with his left hand every other day and with his right hand every other day. At home, he practiced hitting tennis balls against the back wall of the garage, right-handed one day and left-handed the next day. Kyle Gonzalez thought of things to do that no one else ever thought of. But he seemed interested when I told him about horses, interested in a Kyle sort of way, where you knew he was going to go look that up when he got the chance, and then he would put that idea away in his brain somewhere in case he needed it at some future date.

When Jem put the rope around Jack's right ankle, he seemed less able to do what Jem wanted him to do than with the left. The first time, he tried to pull his ankle away, and even reared up a little, but Jem looked like he hardly even noticed. He just held the rope steady until Jack decided to come down again. Then Jack tried to back up, but Jem didn't let him pull his foot away, and so Jack just put it down where it had been before.

Then Jack did a funny thing—he kept his front feet where they were but leaned way back, like he was a cat, stretching. Still, Jem didn't do much. He was waiting for Jack to figure out that stepping forward was easier than trying to get away. There was a long minute, and then Jack picked up the right foot with the rope around it and took a step. Then the other feet followed, and pretty soon, he was walking around the pen, following Jem. He walked fairly evenly, but he never got as smooth as he had on the left—sometimes, he looked down and flicked his ears, as if to say, "What is this thing around my ankle?" It made me laugh.

We must have worked on that for fifteen minutes or so, then Jem put the rope around his neck again and worked him around the pen until he was moving along easily and happily. After he was finished, I put the halter on him and rubbed him down with the chamois. Jem said, "When you're doing that, you could say, 'Shhhh, shhhhh,' in a low voice." When I tried it, Jack put his head down and got really quiet. After a minute or two, it made me feel kind of sleepy, too. I even put my arm over Jack's back and closed my eyes for a second, not something you would think you wanted to do with a colt, but for that second, I felt like we were taking a little bitty nap. Then I smoothed the chamois over his face and around his ears. He yawned twice while I was taking him to the gelding pasture.

Jem Jarrow called out a good-bye, and I thought maybe these lessons were the best we'd ever had, but it is also true that some things you do just get better and better, and every time you do them, it seems like that was the best time ever.

By the time Jack and I were finished, it was starting to get hot, really hot, even though it wasn't ten a.m. when I went back to the house for a glass of water. I saw that Mom had taken the thermometer inside "for a rest," which she sometimes did if she couldn't stand looking at it anymore. She said, "We can feel if it gets above a hundred. We don't have to know it."

She was ready, though—just putting on her boots. I was going to take Lester and she was going to take Lincoln, and we were going to ride down to the crick and back up again. I changed into a T-shirt.

Everything was just normal (though hot) while we were going down to the crick. Mom was in front on Lincoln, who was an easygoing, sure-footed horse, reliable enough so that Mom actually enjoyed riding him, and I was on Lester, who usually had more spirit and wanted to be in the lead but for today had given up all his opinions because of the heat. He was content to plod along behind Lincoln and keep his eye out for the stray leaf or blade of golden grass that he might enjoy. We were almost to the crick when Mom said, "What's that?"

I looked around, but I didn't see anything.

She said, "Over there. Across the crick. It went behind that tree."

I turned my head and saw a movement, but only that. Mom sat up and Lincoln came to a halt. Whatever it was couldn't be much, because the horses didn't care one way or the other. Lester turned his head, and his ears went forward, but his body didn't tense up. And then a head peeked out from behind the tree. It was a brown head with flop ears and a white stripe running up between its eyes. It looked at us and went behind the tree again. Mom said, "Someone's dog! Way out here! That one must be really lost." She urged Lincoln toward the crick and Lester followed. The dog did not appear on either side of the tree. When both horses were standing in the water, Mom put her hand out toward me and said, "Shh."

We waited.

Lester dropped his head and took a drink, then pricked his ears. I saw the dog after he did—it had moved back into the shadows of the trees, but it was still looking at us. When Lincoln snorted, it tensed as if it was going to run away, but then Lincoln didn't move, so the dog didn't move, either.

"Big boy," said Mom. "Looks like a shepherd mix."

We sat there.

Mom loved dogs. My grandfather Jasper Rankin had all kinds of dogs—he would do any type of hunting, but he liked trailing things the best. Usually, it was raccoons, and some of his dogs were coonhounds, but he would trail anything. Once he tracked a little girl who ran away from her kindergarten and got lost, and another time he tracked two men who robbed a bank. Often, in deer-hunting season, someone who wounded a deer but didn't kill it would call my grandfather and have him find the deer. Once, he took his dogs up to Wisconsin and tracked a couple of bears. When I was a little girl in Oklahoma, I was used to being around lots of dogs; once, when I was two, they found me on Christmas afternoon, worn out and sleeping in the back hall among the coonhounds. I'm sure I was very warm, but I didn't remember it.

Daddy liked dogs, too, but he was allergic to them, and so he had never had a dog after he was about seven, and my grandmother and grandfather Lovitt figured out that it was the dogs that were making Daddy wheeze and cough. Once he and Mom got married, my grandparents got a dog again, but whenever Daddy visited them, the dog had to go out to the garage. He was the only person we knew who was allergic to dogs. He couldn't visit my Rankin grandparents at all—they had to come to our house if they wanted to see us.

Mom gave Lincoln a little kick, and he walked to the edge of the crick. He was just about to step up onto the bank, but Mom didn't let him. She leaned forward in the saddle. The dog hadn't moved—in fact, he was sitting, though sitting alertly, as if he *could* move if he had to. Mom said, in a low voice, "Hey, Buddy, hey, Buddy, hey, Buddy." The dog's ears were forward, and he was looking at her. He was as big as a pointer or a retriever, at least. Bigger. Mom said, "What's your name what's your name what's your name." Then she said to me, "Pretty dog. Not a mutt, I don't think."

We watched him for a couple more minutes, then Mom turned Lincoln's head down the crick, and we walked along, over the gravel bed and in the water. It wasn't cool, but the shade of the trees and the splash of the water made it seem not that hot. Mom said, "Look to your right."

I did. The dog was making his way through the trees about twenty feet from the bank, staying out of the sun. When we stopped, the dog stopped. When we started walking again, the dog did, too. Finally, we came to a fence that defined the end of our property—it was barbed wire and built across the crick. That big ranch was on the other side of it, and it prevented Mr. Jordan's cows from coming onto our property. Mom turned and had Lincoln climb the bank. I followed on Lester. We started walking up the hill toward the gelding pasture, and I could see out of the corner of my eye that the dog went down into the crick, took a drink, and then jumped up the bank. As we came up the hill, the dog followed behind. We tried a little trot. The dog trotted after us. We slowed down again. The dog slowed down. We turned to the left and walked along the end of the gelding pasture. The dog first sat down and then, just as we were going around the hill, trotted to catch up. Mom took off her straw hat and then put it on again. Lincoln and Lester kept walking. I turned around and stared at the dog. It was a strange-looking dog, with a hairy face like a terrier and a hairy body. Even though the head had a brown mask with a white blaze, the body was mostly white, with speckles, though there was one brown spot, like a lopsided saddle, over his back. He followed us all the way up the hill and then sat down just beyond the buildings, staring at us. After we had put the horses away and come back out of the barn, he was still sitting there. The geldings were looking at him, and so were the mares, but they didn't seem nervous. Mom said, "I think that dog has been here before." Then she said, "I think we have a dog."

That was a good thought.

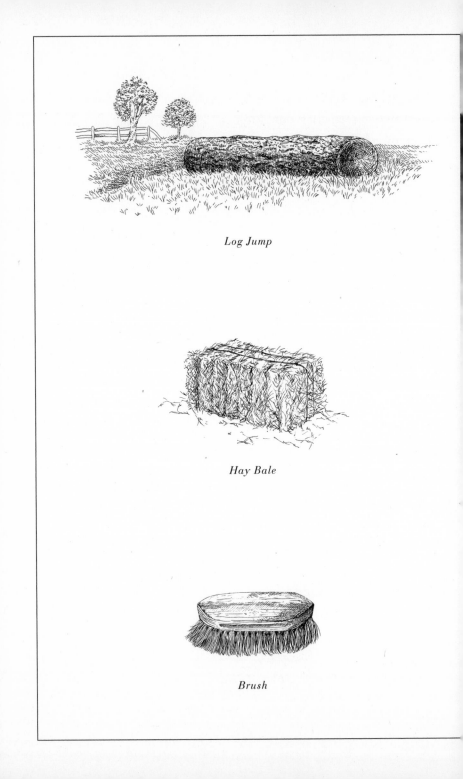

Log Jump

Hay Bale

Brush

Chapter 3

I am sure Daddy saw the dog, too, since for the next few days, if I looked in the right direction, I would see it there, usually sitting and looking back at me. If you drew a circle around the barn and the house and Mom's garden and Jack's old pen, that would be the circle the dog did not enter, but at any time it could be just outside that circle, lying down, sitting, walking, making itself at home. I almost had the feeling that the more it walked around the circle looking at us, the more we started to belong to it, in its own mind, but it was being cautious and thinking if it entered the circle too soon, it would be kicked out, and it would have been. Mom and I didn't mention the dog because we knew that the only chance of having it around was Daddy getting used to it, and having no one to argue with about it. The dog would of course never come into the house. But maybe it could, someday, come into the barn.

On Monday after Jem Jarrow had given me my second lesson, I came home from school to discover that Daddy had set up as good a jumping course as he could in the arena, and that Black George was all tacked up and waiting for me. I went right in the house to change into my riding clothes, and as I did, Daddy called, "Bring out that list!"

He meant the list I had made of the things I was supposed to do when I was jumping a course. Sometimes, he made me go over that list line by line, just to make sure that we were getting the most out of our times with Miss Slater. I put on my boots and found the list in my horse notebook. The weather had broken; it was about fifteen degrees cooler than it had been, so I knew we had plenty of work to do.

Daddy was holding Black George, and I handed him the list, which he read while I recited:

"Ride the course, not the jumps."

"What does that mean?"

"Well, if I think of the jumps too much, I will look at each one and forget to go forward, but if I think of where I'm going, the jumps will get jumped automatically."

"Okay. Number 2."

"Keep the horse level, especially through the corners."

"What does that mean?"

"I have to sit up and a little back, and make sure that his front legs are moving evenly and his shoulders are the same height."

"Why?"

"Because he could slip otherwise, or come into a jump off-balance."

"Okay. Three."

"Look ahead ten strides, not two or five."

"That's about . . ."

"That's about keeping going, like the first one, but also about being prepared and knowing where you are going."

"Four."

"Ride to the middle of every fence."

"Why?"

"Because getting to the middle is hard, but if you try to get there, there's a better chance you will at least get close."

"Yes," said Daddy. "And also, the horse can't see the fence as you approach it, because his eyes are set to either side of his head. If you ride to the middle of the fence, he has a better sense of where he is and when and how to jump."

"He can't see the fence?"

"Not while he's jumping it."

I didn't know what to think about this. It was a little scary. On the other hand, Black George didn't seem to care whether he could see the fence or not—he was always right about where it was. I said, "Okay."

"Five?"

"Wait."

"How can you wait when you are galloping?"

"Well, I don't want to get my body in front of the horse's body. I am waiting for him rather than leaning out ahead of him. Also, his strides should be even, so I don't want to get him to change his strides by making him go faster."

"Good. You sound like you've passed this test before."

"I have. Six is like five: maintain a rhythm."

"Why is that?"

"Nobody gets nervous."

"Right—"

"Or, if somebody is nervous, the other one doesn't realize it."

Daddy laughed.

I said, "Seven should be one. Look up, never down."

"Why is that?"

"'Cause if you look down, you can fall down."

"But also . . ."

"When you are looking down, you are looking at the jumps and riding the jumps, not the course. When you are looking up, you are riding the course, not the jumps."

"Okay!" said Daddy. "A-plus!" And he threw me onto Black George.

He must have spent the whole afternoon setting up the course, because he had also taken the tractor and dragged the entire arena. The sand was grooved and even all around. There were eight jumps, and every one of them even weirder than usual.

They weren't all that high, but Black George and I had never seen any of them quite like this before. Daddy had set out three hay bales end to end and on top of them arranged a row of books. A few strides past that was a pair of stools holding up a two-by-four or something like that, with four pairs of his jeans hanging over them. At the far curve of the arena was the picket fence he liked to use, but with branches woven between the pickets. He had dragged in a log from somewhere—it was higher on the sides than in the middle, which would make us jump the middle. There were three sawhorses set end to end, their legs wrapped in Christmas ribbon. A row of Mom's Mexican pots with flowers growing out of them. A row of kitchen chairs, but with one of my stuffed animals sitting in each seat—panda, giraffe, Raggedy Ann, floppy dog, rabbit. The last one was almost regular—he had taken a pair of jump standards that we had and set three poles across it, but he had dangled kitchen spoons from the top pole so that they clanked against the poles beneath.

I figured I should be nervous, but Black George trotted around and past all of these scary things without blinking, hardly flicking his ears. I guess he knew Daddy was capable of anything.

The point here was to train a jumper the way you would train a parade horse or a police horse. Daddy had trained a lot of parade horses, who then had to handle things like Fourth of July parades and the Shriners coming to town and the rodeo. You never knew what people were going to do at a parade, partly because you had to assume that, as Mom said, some people enjoyed the parade by going to bars ahead of time. So, there could be kids running around, firecrackers going off, yelling, flags waving, balloons, cars honking, banners flapping, not to mention brass bands and baton twirling. Daddy's idea about a jumper was that a horse show might look a little quieter than a parade, but you never knew, best to take precautions. So I wound in and out of the jumps, trotting and then cantering, and for Black George, it was just a stroll through the park. A quiet park.

The jumps were set around the arena like this:

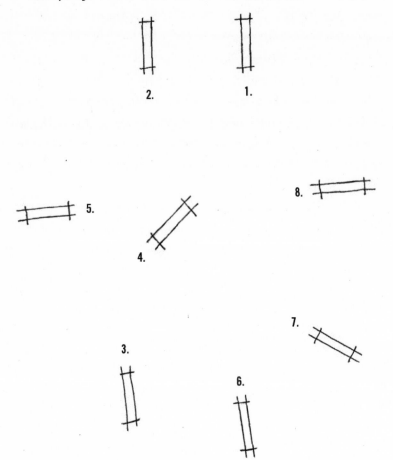

My first job was to jump back and forth over 1 and 2, the books and the flowerpots, a few times, making sure that Black George took a stride between the jumps. This was a "one-stride in-and-out." Once we did that (and Daddy already had a big smile because Black George was jumping carefully but happily over these two), we went over the books and the flowers and then down and around and over 3, the picket fence. Then I went over the first three again and then around number 7, the blue jeans, and back over number 6, the kitchen chairs with Freddie, Floppy, Peanut, Raggedy Ann, and Nubbin the bunny. Black George was enjoying himself and I was getting excited. The next step was to go down over number 4, the poles and spoons, then around 2 and 1, and back over 8, the sawhorses, and 7, the jeans, then around 6 to 5, the log. There were no tight turns, and Black George galloped in a relaxed way. Since the jumps weren't high, I just stayed with him, feeling him rise up under me, then gallop away. It was very easy to ride the course. But the course was small, and only two turns.

The next thing was to jump everything in order—1 and 2, the in-and-out, around to 3, right-hand loop around the 7, then down over the 4. Left-hand turn around the 2, down over the 5, bend around the 3, and up over the 6, then a tight turn to the 7, and finish over the 8. That was three curves and two tight turns. I sat on Black George, who was breathing a little hard but had his ears pricked, and studied the course, first actually pointing with my finger and saying "1, 2, 3 . . . ," then turning my head and staring at each jump in order. Just then it seemed like a long time since I took Melinda's pony in the horse show, and I felt a surge of tension right in the front of my chest. But Black George was ready to go.

I began to circle him at the trot, but almost immediately, he lifted on his own into a bouncy canter. I turned him toward number 1, the books. I said to myself only one thing: "Go to the corner. Go to the corner." But I said it as if I were counting the syllables along with his strides—GO to the CORner. GO to the CORner. First 1, 2, 3, back around to 4, out and around to 5, down over 6, then 7, then 8, then ease down to the trot.

Daddy was smiling, and he shouted, "Beautiful, Abby!" But I barely cared what he was shouting. I was thrilled in myself and happy with Black George, as if he had given me a present.

Then we did it again. It was less exciting this time, and that was a good thing. I felt that my attitude about jumping the course was more like Black George's now—having fun, no big deal. There are ways in which you can feel dumber than your horse—he knows what you are doing better than you know it, so it is a little embarrassing to have made such a big deal over something he considers part of his job, and rather routine.

This was not a way I usually felt about the horses—usually, I assumed that I knew more than they did. Daddy *always* assumed that he knew more than they did. But it was also true that when Danny was a little kid, and Mom and Daddy lived back in Oklahoma, Daddy had a cutting horse mare who worked the cattle without a bridle. As a trick, once, he took her into a ring with several calves and reached forward and pulled off her bridle. She did all her work—separating a calf, moving him, cornering him—with Daddy just sitting there holding on to her mane to keep his balance. After that first time, he did it fairly often, he said, just showing off. I bet the mare liked it— when we asked him about it, he said that he could never teach any other cutting horses to do that—the mare learned that on her own and maybe knew more than Daddy could have taught her. At any rate, after our work with Black George, we felt like he would be ready to go to the show grounds and jump over everything.

In the next few days, Mom said nothing about the dog, and I didn't, either. We could see it out there, trotting or walking around, taking care of its business, whatever that was. Twice, I saw it sitting alertly, staring at the horses, once at the mares and once at the geldings, but I didn't think anything of it—I stared at the horses myself, because horses are interesting. But a few days after Black George and I had our great lesson, Mom and Daddy and I were sitting at supper talking about the show when we suddenly heard lots of high whinnies and then galloping feet. Normally, the horses would be quietly eating their evening hay, so Daddy jumped up from the table, and Mom and I were right after him. We ran out of the house.

The first thing we saw was the mares, all standing in a line, staring toward the geldings. You couldn't see the geldings from the front of the house, but once we could see them, there was the dog, speckled white with a brown head, chasing Jack and Lester, or Jack or Lester, down the long side of the pasture, fast and silent, not barking, its head low and intent. Lester turned suddenly, and the dog kept on—Jack was the prey. Mom gasped, and Daddy said, "Lord have mercy!"

We ran toward the fence, and Daddy started shouting, "Hey! Hey, you mutt! Lay off!" He picked up a stone, and when we got to the fence, he threw it. It hit the dog on the rump and startled it. Mom said, "Oh dear." The dog stopped running and turned to look at us. Jack stopped running, too, and though I had thought he was afraid, I now wondered, because he swept around the end of the pasture in a big trot and started back toward the dog, snorting but with his ears pricked.

43

Then he stopped. His nostrils were flaring, but he seemed more excited than worried.

Daddy said, "I saw this dog around." He shook his head. Mom and I exchanged a glance, and I wondered if maybe she had made better friends with the dog than I knew about. She said, "I can't believe he thinks Jack is prey."

"He doesn't think anything," said Daddy. "He sees something move and chases it. You can tell by the way his hind end is built that there's something fast in there, some coursing breed."

But Jack flipped his tail and whinnied, as if to get the dog to play. I took a couple of steps toward the gate, thinking I would catch him and walk him around. The dog by this time was standing with his head turned toward Mom, and I think Daddy was having a few thoughts of his own about why the dog was looking at Mom—and if he wasn't, he should have been—when a funny thing happened. Jefferson walked up to the dog and without even sniffing him or getting acquainted in any way, bent his knees against the dog's side and rolled him over. Before he knew it, the dog was lying on his back, looking up at Jefferson, who was looking down at him. And the dog didn't scramble to his feet. He waited for Jefferson to step back, which Jefferson did, eventually, and then the dog got to his feet, head down, tail low, and slunk away. Daddy laughed. Mom said, "I never saw that before. How did Jefferson know that? That's what you do to show a dog you're the boss."

I said, "Do horses do that to each other?"

"Never saw it," said Daddy.

Jefferson might as well have slapped his hands together,

congratulating himself on a job well done—that was the look on his face as he walked away. He touched noses with Lester, touched noses with Jack, and touched noses with Lincoln, then he trotted to a nice pile of hay and gave himself a reward. The dog, still evidently embarrassed, made his way to the far end of the gelding pasture and slipped under the bottom railing of the fence. Then he disappeared over the brow of the hill.

"Good riddance," said Daddy.

Mom didn't say anything.

Daddy said, "I guess we should put the food we leave out for the barn cats up high somewhere. That's probably what the dog is looking for."

"Probably," said Mom. "But I'm not giving them anything much, just some leftover vegetables and some bread."

"If he's starving, that will be enough to attract him."

"If he's starving . . ." But she didn't finish her sentence. Daddy was strict about loose dogs. If they were going to live like foxes or bobcats, they had to live like them and kill their own food. We wouldn't leave food out for a bobcat, would we? If a cougar couldn't make it on his own, we wouldn't encourage him to come by for a meal, would we? Wild was wild, and there was no use pretending it wasn't. And a stray dog could have distemper or even rabies. Mom and I knew all of these things. But it was a nice dog. Running, you could even say it was a beautiful dog that could use a bath and a brushing. But we didn't say anything. Daddy checked over Lester and I checked over Jack, and then we went in the house and finished our supper.

Water Jump

Coop in Fence Line

Double Crossbar Jump

Chapter 4

ON SATURDAY, WE LOADED BLACK GEORGE INTO THE (NEWLY washed) trailer and drove him, with the (newly washed) truck, out to the stable where Miss Slater worked. It was sunny when we left home, a bright, warmish day, perfect for riding, but as soon as we turned toward the coast, we could see a bank of fog lying like a gray pillow over exactly the spot we were headed toward. It made me shiver just to look at it. But Mom had sent along an extra sweater, so I knew I would be fine. Miss Slater had never seen Black George before, so we gave him a bath, pulled his mane, and combed out his tail, which was long and luxurious. I had also cleaned the saddle and bridle. We had not clipped the insides of his ears or his whiskers. Daddy said that a horse living out needed the hair in his ears to keep flies away and the whiskers to find the grass. He kept a straight face as he said this, but I laughed, anyway.

On the way over, I did some homework. We had lots more homework in eighth grade than seventh, and sometimes, it was hard to fit it in. I had a book report due Monday about *Great Expectations*. I had not been able to make head or tail of *Great Expectations*, partly because I kept dozing off when I was trying to read it. I thought if I read while we were driving, I might stay awake. Our next book after *Great Expectations* was going to be a play, *Julius Caesar*. Alexis and Barbara Goldman had decided that in order to get through it, some of us were going to come over to their house and read it out loud, but I had to make something of *Great Expectations* first. As we were driving through the damp pines, I could just get glimpses of the ocean from time to time, and I tried to imagine a big old boat sitting out there, with a family living in it like a cabin, which is something that happens in *Great Expectations*. I couldn't.

Miss Slater was finishing up with a lesson—a girl on a chestnut pony cantering around the ring with a determined look on her face. At one point, the pony slowed down, and the girl smacked him a good one with the whip. The pony sped up, with his ears pinned, but the girl stayed on, and the pony kept going. When they were finished, Miss Slater said, "That child is only seven, and I think this is her sixth lesson, but she keeps her heels down, and she *is* determined. So, let's see the young man."

She was referring to Black George. Daddy backed him out of the trailer and took off his lightweight blanket (which we had also washed). Miss Slater went, "Hmmmm." But it was a long *hmm*, which went from well-I-wonder-what-they've-come-up-with-now to my-goodness!

Black George hadn't been away from our place in months—not since Daddy brought him in from Oklahoma—so you would expect him to look bright, and maybe be a little nervous, but he stood quietly and evenly on all four legs, his neck arched and his ears pricked. When Miss Slater stepped up to him and began to run her hands over him, he sniffed her curiously but not impolitely (a curious horse is always better than a nervous horse) and then gave a sigh. She said, "How does he jump?"

"I guess we'll see," said Daddy.

We saddled him up and led him to one of the back rings, not one of the show rings, but nice, on the edge of the forest. I noticed that the little girl came along and climbed on the railings to watch. She still had that serious look on her face. Miss Slater called out to her, "Ellen! Don't make your mom look for you again!"

Ellen shouted, "It's okay!" She didn't move. I had to smile.

There were only about five jumps in the arena, all standards and poles except for one white panel, but there was a chicken coop along the fence line, and out past that one I could see some jumps in a field. Miss Slater called, "Let's see his trot!"

I thought about Jem Jarrow for a moment, then tweaked the inside rein just enough for Black George to lift his inside shoulder and step his inside hind a little in front of his outside hind. His whole body got lighter and more supple, and his chin tucked. We trotted a circle to the right and then a circle to the left, then straight down the long side of the arena, stretching out a bit. At the end of the arena, I just squeezed my fingers and he came right back to me, shortening his step. Then I crossed the arena in front of Miss Slater and Daddy and asked

Black George for a canter. He was happy to oblige. It went like this for maybe ten minutes, me trying to be Jem Jarrow, and Black George just being his perfect self. I was glad that, of all the geldings, he seemed to be Jack's best friend; I hoped his good nature would rub off a little bit.

While I rode Black George (and Ellen stood on the fence, staring at me as hard as she could), Daddy and Miss Slater moved the jump standards and paced out the distance between them. I could see that Daddy was watching Miss Slater and asking her a few questions. Pretty soon, they had everything set up.

There were five jumps in a much simpler pattern than we'd had at home, just two along one long side, and then another two, farther apart, along the other long side. The fifth jump was set diagonally almost but not quite in the middle of the arena. There were two verticals—just poles, like a fence; an oxer, which is two verticals right together, the one in front lower and the one in back higher, really just a wide jump; and the panel hanging between two standards. The jump across the center was a double crossbar—that is, like an oxer but made of two sets of crossed poles.

Miss Slater told me to circle at one end of the arena, then trot down over the double crossbar, which was very low, about a foot high and a foot wide, and then halt, turn, and canter back over the jump. Black George did this well, took each pair of jumps, vertical to oxer, then took the second pair backward (though Miss Slater adjusted the fence), oxer to vertical. No problem. Black George was ready for the whole course.

It was easy—eight jumps: down over 1 to 2, through the middle, around 3 and back over it, then a wide turn at the end of the

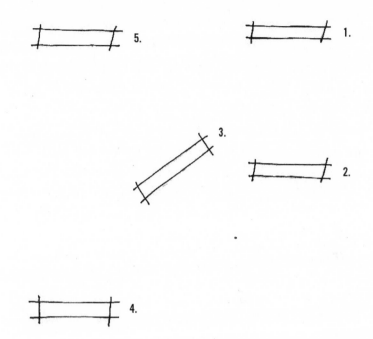

arena, and up over 4 and 5. Short turn back over 3, another short turn over 5, and around the end and down over 1, except that I got confused after 5 the first time, lost my way, and had to stop, because the course went from looking like five jumps set in a pattern to looking like a bowl of spaghetti. I came to a halt.

Miss Slater said, "You had this problem last spring. Just take your time and look at the turns." She lifted her hand and made two of her fingers walk. Then she turned toward the jumps and held her hand up and walked her fingers through the air around the course. Then she looked at me and waited. Finally, I did the same thing. As soon as I started to do it, I could see Daddy out of the corner of my eye, nodding his head. But I felt like an idiot.

It worked, though. I got over the course, and I sat up in

the corners, and when I was finished, Ellen shouted, "Hurray!" and Miss Slater said, "Very good." Then she and Daddy put the jumps up. When Miss Slater was putting the jump up over by Ellen, she talked to her very strongly. Ellen looked at her and then shook her head. I was walking Black George around, and I couldn't help smiling. I went over the course again. This time the jumps were higher, but still not terribly high, maybe three feet. Black George couldn't have been having a better time. When I brought him down to the walk and walked past Ellen, she yelled, "I want that horse! Is that horse for sale? I love him! Stop! I want to pat him!"

I stopped by the fence. She stretched out her hand and stroked his neck. Miss Slater marched over and stood in front of Ellen with her hands on her hips. She said, "Ellen Leinsdorf! You are being very naughty! Please don't make me take you back to the big ring! I'm sure your mother is looking all over for you!"

The expression on Ellen's face said, "Let her look." Just then, Daddy walked over and stood in front of Ellen. Daddy was not smiling, and I knew he was going to come up with something about honoring thy father and mother and "Obey your parents in everything, for this pleases the Lord," but instead, he said, "Ellen, how about if I walk you over to the parking lot, and if your mother is there, we can ask her to come over here and watch the horse." Ellen jumped down from the fence and slid through it, between the two bottom slats. She might have been the smallest seven-year-old I'd ever seen. She put her hand in Daddy's, which surprised him, and they started walking. As they crossed the arena, I could hear her talking a mile a minute. Miss Slater said, "She's not a naughty child, but she is stubborn as a tree stump. Now, Abby, while they're gone, let's try some flying changes."

Black George and I had worked on these, and when I paid attention, he was good. Even so, he was comfortable with whatever lead he happened to be on, no matter what direction he was going in, so there was no reason to change. I explained this to Miss Slater.

"Well, Abby, he may not have a reason to change, but you do. The canter is an asymmetrical gait, and the legs launch and then catch the horse. If he's on the proper lead—if his outside hind launches the step, then the inside hind and outside fore-leg continue it, and finally the inside foreleg catches it. The inside foreleg steps farther forward so that the outside hind can come under and launch again. If he's on the proper lead, his path to each jump will be straighter, safer, and also more in line with how the course designer has set it up. You want him to get to the jump and over it in the easiest way, and that means changing leads when he turns away from the direction he's been going in."

She had me sit up straight and canter to the left, in a large loop. When I came across my path again, I was to use my right leg to get him to move a little sideways to the right, and touch him behind the saddle with my right heel. We knew he could change leads, the question was whether he would. Left to right was easier, and he did do it. It felt like a four-footed hop that then smoothed into a right-lead canter. I stopped him, and we did it again. Then we tried exactly the same thing starting to the right and changing to the left. We were both more awkward at this. I didn't sit up very straight, and he only changed his front legs. Miss Slater was patient. We tried again, me thinking, "Sit up! Sit up! One—sit up; two—move him over; three—touch him with the left heel!" He changed, and more smoothly than the times to the right, as if it wasn't such a big deal. We tried again, missed again, then tried again, and had a good one.

Miss Slater said, "It's very much a question of being sensitive to the rhythm of the horse's stride. Count the steps, sit up, ask for the change." While I was thinking of this, Daddy returned without Ellen Leinsdorf. The look on his face said, "So long, it's been good to know you," which was an old song he sang around the barn sometimes. Miss Slater didn't ask him anything about it.

Instead, she pointed to the jumps in the field and said, "Abby, we are rather proud of our outside course, and I think you might like going over a few of those. I'm sure Black George will enjoy the open space, and most of those are fairly modest." We walked to the coop in the fence line and gazed out across the field, which maybe in the spring was green but now was a bright, clipped golden color. There were six different obstacles out there—three fences made of living green bushes, a big log, an actual stone wall, a long slope that ended abruptly in a vertical bank that looked pretty high to me (you could jump on or off this anywhere along the slope, so your jump could be any height from about one foot to bigger than I could imagine jumping up to or down from). From where we stood, they seemed randomly scattered in the field. Miss Slater climbed over the fence beside the coop, and Daddy climbed after her.

When they were out there, she shouted, "Make a circle and jump the coop. It's a very inviting fence!"

And so it was.

We walked toward the center of the field. Now the jumps seemed to be more in a pattern. One that I hadn't noticed before and certainly would avoid was a big ditch full of water. Since the sun had come out, the water looked deep and blue. The ground sloped up to it slightly; then there was a narrow small log; and then the rippling water, which looked very wide; and another very narrow log defining the other side.

The first thing I did was jump on and off the sides of the bank. They were very low—not more than one foot high or two feet high. Black George hesitated going down at first, but only to figure out how to balance with me on him—he and the other geldings went in and out of our crick all the time, on their own and with us on their backs. The brush fences were fun, too. Miss Slater was all smiles.

Finally, she gave me a course—do a canter circle to the right, jump back into the ring and over the red and white vertical poles, then come out again over the coop. Gallop down over the first brush going away, then the second brush coming back. Then take the bank crosswise—up one side about halfway along the slope, then two strides across and down the other side, then turn right and come back to where they were standing.

I gathered the reins. I did not close one eye, lift my hand, and walk my fingers around over the jumps. What could be hard? Over the coop, over the red and white poles, back out over the coop, out to the brush, back over the other brush, then around and up the bank, down the bank, to the left, and back. Except that I didn't realize just how happy Black George would be when he came back out over the coop. I did not expect him to take hold of the bit and go a little fast over the first brush and then a little faster over the second brush. I did not know that the tears in my eyes were from speed—I thought they were from the breeze. When we headed for the bank, his ears were pricked—what an easy thing to do! Up! Down! Just like that! And then he galloped on. I let him, because we didn't get to gallop in such a beautiful, gently rolling field very often. And then I turned left.

The trouble with left and right is that you have a fifty-fifty chance of being wrong. So when I turned left at a brisk gallop, there we were, maybe five or six strides out from the giant ditch (it looked as big as our whole crick), and Black George was going fast. I saw his ears prick, and then, before I knew it, he had shifted his weight backward—not in order to stop (and maybe dump me in the water) but in order to gather himself and leap. When I realized that that was what he was doing, I grabbed his mane, pushed my heels down, and more or less curled up on his neck and went with him. He landed and galloped on. Fortunately, there weren't any more jumps between me and Daddy and Miss Slater, who were now standing on the bank, staring toward me. I brought Black George around in a circle and stopped beside the bank. I was panting harder than the horse was.

Miss Slater said, "How old is that horse? Where did you get that horse?"

Daddy said, "He's five, as far as we know. We thought he

was four, but his teeth seem to be those of a five-year-old. I got him in Oklahoma."

There was a long pause while I walked Black George around in a circle. I didn't know if I was in trouble or not.

Miss Slater said, "He didn't put a toe in the water."

"How wide is it?" said Daddy. I could tell he was trying to remain calm.

"Well . . . ," said Miss Slater.

There was another pause. Black George and I kept walking in our circle.

"Well." She coughed. "There is a constant argument around here about that water jump. It's too big, and I keep telling the colonel—"

"How wide is it?" said Daddy.

"The colonel insisted on, I must say, fifteen feet. Including the little logs." Then she said, "I myself have never jumped it. The widest I've ever jumped is twelve feet."

We were quiet for a long time after that, then Daddy said, "Abby, why didn't you stop?"

I said, "Black George didn't want to stop."

Daddy said, "Sometimes, a horse isn't the best judge of what to do."

I said, "I know that. I'm sorry." But I was only sorry about part of it—what might have happened. I wasn't at all sorry about what did happen—being in the air over that big water and knowing that Black George was enjoying himself maybe more than he ever had was the thrill of my life. We all walked back to the main stable grounds without saying anything. I had Black George on a loose rein, and he was swinging his head and neck, looking here and there. His nostrils were flaring, but he didn't seem tired. Every so often, Miss Slater, who was walking beside us, would turn and look at him, then pat him on the neck. When we got back to the trailer, she pulled a sugar cube out of her pocket and gave it to him, saying, "Well, you are a fine fellow, Black George. I would love to know your breeding."

Then she and Daddy talked about the show, which was to begin in five days, on Thursday, but because of school, we wouldn't be coming over until Saturday. We were entered in two classes on Saturday, nice, easy hunter classes. These were like the ones I had ridden Gallant Man in the previous spring—the horse was to jump nicely and show good manners, but the jumps were not terribly big, and the courses didn't have a lot of turns. We tied Black George to the trailer and untacked him, then brushed him down. I thought the weather was too cool to hose him off—we could do that at home, where it would be sunny and warm. When he was all clean and relaxed, Daddy loaded him in the trailer and we headed for home.

Daddy was saying nothing in a very suspicious way—in exactly the way he usually got when he was hatching a plan. It was always, always better when Daddy talked. I looked at him a couple of times, waiting for him to say something, but then, when he didn't, I picked up *Great Expectations* again. It wasn't until we were almost home that I realized that I had put the bookmark in the wrong spot, and I was reading a section I had already read without even knowing it. Right when I noticed that, Daddy suddenly said, "Did that jump really come as a surprise to you? You galloped right past it."

"I don't know why I didn't see it, except that the sun wasn't shining on it. I don't know."

"Let's not tell your mother how big it was, okay?"

"It wasn't as hard as it looked. I just curled up and sat there. He did all the work."

"He surely did. He surely did. But thank the Lord you stuck on."

I nodded.

Because of church, I wasn't allowed to do homework on Sunday. The Sabbath was reserved for the Lord, and we went to church all day with our Brothers and Sisters. We could feed the horses, of course, and cook for the church supper, but we could not engage in "secular pursuits." Therefore, I had to sit in my room that night and finish reading *Great Expectations* and then write my book report in ink, because I didn't have time to copy it over for Monday. I had no idea what to say, so I did a funny thing—I imagined that I was Kyle Gonzalez and just started writing. I imagined Kyle going on and on about everything in *Great Expectations* that no one else in the world cared about, like what did the author mean by naming a character Magwitch, and why did he name the main boy Pip and the old woman Havisham? I came up with some Kyle-ish ideas, for two and a half pages, and put it away and that was that! It was pretty easy, in the end.

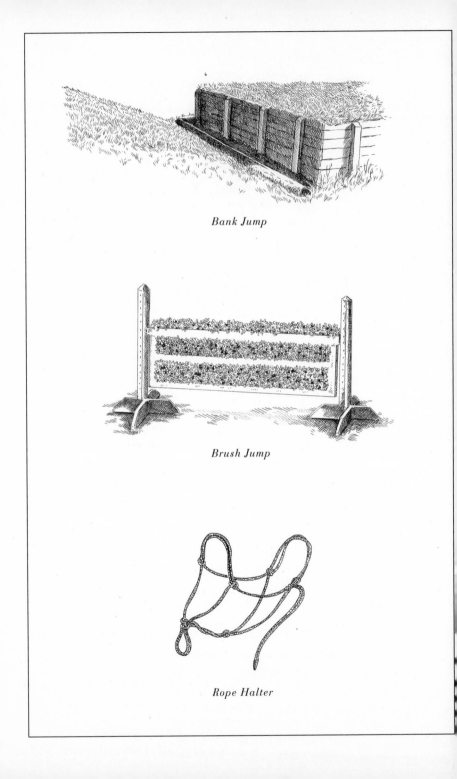

Bank Jump

Brush Jump

Rope Halter

Chapter 5

ON MONDAY, THERE WAS ANOTHER LETTER FROM MR. BRANDT in Texas. Daddy showed it to me after dinner. It read:

Dear Mr. Lovitt,

Thank you for your prompt reply. Since I last wrote you, I have interviewed Mr. Robert Hogarth again, and also I have twice spoken to Mrs. Hogarth (who, you may know, does the correspondence and bookkeeping for By Golly Horse Sales). Most important, I finally managed to get in touch with Mr. Samuel Walker, who, you may remember, was temporarily managing the sale barn when you visited in November, while Mr. Hogarth was recuperating from an illness. I had not spoken to

Mr. Walker before, because he has moved from Oklahoma to Florida, but I have now talked to him over the telephone and in person.

While we cannot be one hundred percent certain that the mare you purchased was Alabama Lady, the profile of the mare who came into By Golly Horse Sales and was sold to you fits the profile of Alabama Lady in color, size, and condition. The Hogarths did not suspect that the mare was pregnant, and neither did Sam Walker, though he does remember wondering how she could be very bony and also have such a big belly, but he thought it was just a hay belly. Alabama Lady was a big-boned, rangy mare, long in the back, and perhaps her pregnancy was not as apparent as it might have been in a more compact animal. I have written to two others who bought brown mares from By Golly Horse Sales in November and December. I have heard from one of these parties—that mare has not produced a foal. I am waiting to hear from the other party.

If your mare was indeed Alabama Lady, then the foal you have is a valuable one. Alabama Lady's first foal, a colt, is now a four-year-old. He has won a stakes race in Arkansas. Her second foal, also a colt, is a three-year-old, who has won four races, including two stakes, in California. The two-year-old filly is promising, too. Most important, the sire of the foal Alabama Lady was carrying is a horse named Jaipur, who won the Belmont Stakes and the Travers Stakes in 1962 (as you may remember). He is the best horse Alabama Lady has been bred to, and his stud fee last year was substantial. Alabama Lady was sent to Kentucky to breed with Jaipur and returned when she was four months in foal.

Please let me know if you have come up with any other information concerning your purchase of the horse. I would very much like to see any paperwork pertaining to her, or perhaps you took a photograph of her when she arrived in California?

Yours truly,
Howard W. Brandt

I read the letter very calmly, I thought. He still wasn't saying, Your horse is mine, give me back my horse. There was still the chance that this other brown mare that passed through the sale barn was exactly like Brown Jewel (or Pearl) in every possible way and that she produced a big, beautiful brown colt with a cowlick in the middle of his forelock who moved like a . . . panther? a deer? In fact, like a racehorse. There was still that chance. I said, "What do you think that he means by *substantial?*"

"You mean the stud fee," said Daddy. "Do you know what a stud fee is?"

"I can imagine," I said.

"Well, don't imagine too hard," said Mom.

I think this was meant to be a joke.

Daddy said, "Over a thousand dollars, anyway. I don't know too much about it, but these are rich people, very rich people, people who are richer maybe than we can imagine, so we don't know what they would pay for something they wanted."

"Are you saying that if they can prove that Brown Jewel was Alabama Lady, and we want to keep Jack, they would make us pay that kind of money for him?"

"They might. Why wouldn't they?" said Daddy. "How do you think they got rich? It wasn't by doing favors. Jesus said that it is harder for a rich man to get into heaven than for a camel to pass through the eye of a needle."

Mom lowered her voice. "At this point, we don't know anything about what they suspect or intend, but your daddy and I would like to be prepared."

"You mean I should be prepared, because I'm the one who cares."

"Are you sassing me?" said Daddy. He cleared his throat.

"I don't know," I said. "I'm saying what I think." But I was not saying all of what I thought. I thought that he would be glad to get rid of my horse, whose birth had been a surprise, and who was too young to be saleable or useful, and that when I wasn't around, he was breathing that old sigh of relief—the Lord had intervened, and it was all for the best, and thank you, Jesus. *All* of what I thought was pretty angry.

I went to my room and did my homework. I was finished with *Great Expectations*, but there were plenty of stupid equations, a pile of junk about three types of muscle fiber, some pointless reading about crops of the temperate zones, and *je ne sais quoi* about *tout le monde*. It took me the rest of the night, but it didn't put me to sleep. What did put me to sleep was the idea of disappearing with Jack. There were ranches all around us with plenty of grass for him. I could take a blanket and sleep on the ground. And then I thought about snakes and mountain lions and coyotes, but I dropped off, anyway.

When I woke up, I was still mad, but I knew I needed a better plan than walking away with Jack across the crick and over the mountains. When I got to school, the first thing I said to Gloria was, "Your mom really likes Jack, doesn't she?"

"Oh, she loves him," said Gloria. We were in the bathroom, and she was putting on lipstick, but she wasn't using the mirror. Gloria had practiced putting on lipstick so many times that she could do a perfect job just by feel. She pressed her lips together and then blotted them. She said, "I love him, too. You are so lucky."

"I'm not lucky if those people from Texas come to get him."

"Well, you bought the mare fair and square. I'm sure your dad can get the money back for her, and then he can give it to those people, and they will sell you Jack."

"You think so?" Now she was combing her hair. She was good at doing that without a mirror, too, but I said, "Why don't you ever look in the mirror?"

"Because you just see yourself backward. How you look in a mirror is not how you really look. I decided not to get used to thinking that is the way I look. My mom got this new Polaroid Swinger camera. Have you seen one of those? After I get ready in the morning, I take my picture, and it develops right there, and so I know what I really look like. I think it's a great idea, even if I do say so myself."

"Maybe your mom would buy a horse."

"You mean Jack."

"If we didn't have enough to buy him."

Gloria stopped fixing herself and looked at me. Then she smiled. She said, "I think that would be fun."

"Well, don't say anything yet. There's still the chance that another mare was the stolen mare." But I didn't really believe that.

When I got home from school that afternoon, I went to Jack first. With all the horses we had, I was only working with Jack about every three or four days, but Jem Jarrow thought that was fine, because Jack also had to have plenty of time just to be a horse and to grow up. The other geldings sometimes looked as though they wished he *would* grow up—for example, when he played by rearing up and putting his front legs on one of them.

And only Black George would let Jack share his hay. If he came up to one of the others when that one was eating, the horse would pin his ears and chase him off, sometimes with a nip or two. I also noticed that if they were all standing by the gate and I had an apple or a piece of bread, if I held it out to Jack, Jefferson or Lester would push in and insist that I give it to them. So I made sure to cut the apples and break the bread into enough pieces for everyone. That afternoon, I gave them all some bread, then I snapped the rope onto Jack's halter and led him out. All I planned to do was give him a good brushing and work with his feet, since Jake Morrisson would be there that weekend to trim him. Danny would be coming, too, and I was sure that Danny would have some idea about the people in Texas.

Jack must have been reading my mind. Sometimes, a horse reads your mind and doesn't like what he sees in there, I guess. Anyway, Jack started misbehaving almost immediately—he was pushy on the lead line and kept getting ahead of me, so that I had to do what Jem had told me and stand in front of him and insist that he step backward. The first time, he was so resistant that I had to pop him with the rope under his chin, which I hadn't had to do in months. Then, every two or three steps, I had to halt him and insist that he halt when I halted. Of course he moved his feet, so I had to make myself be strict and mean what I said, and not move on until he had actually stopped moving his feet and relaxed. After doing this three times (plus the popping), I was feeling bored and therefore impatient. I couldn't believe that after all this time, he still wasn't leading properly, when there were so many other things that were more fun that we might have been doing instead of me leading him from the gelding pasture to the pen.

Then I stopped again, and he stopped, and I turned my head to look at him. His head was cocked in my direction, and his ears were forward. His eye caught my eye, and his nostril flared, and I thought at that moment that he was utterly beautiful, the most beautiful horse I ever saw, and also he was a baby, hardly bigger, in his way, than I was. His hooves were small, his legs were thin and long, his body was wiry, and his mane was just a line of hairs standing up along his neck, about halfway between fuzz and real black hairs. He was unbelievably cute, and I reached out and stroked him on his neck, at which point he lifted up on his hind legs, easy as pie.

He was a baby. Well, maybe he was more of a toddler. I waited for Jack to come down (a long second), and then I remembered Jem saying that there are things we simply ignore, and I walked toward the gate again, stopping twice. Jack stopped with me both times. He even waited quietly while I opened the gate and then led him through it.

I undid the lead rope and let him trot away.

In the pen, he made me a little nervous, though, especially when he began squealing, pawing, and kicking as he trotted and galloped around me. The squeals were sharp and short, as if he were angry—he would pin his ears, let out a high squeal, and in the middle of it kick out, or twist into the air, or throw his shoulders to one side and paw the air, then he would run three strides and stand up on his hind legs. And he didn't always stick to the periphery of the pen—sometimes, he would cross pretty close to me as if he didn't know I was there, or didn't care. He ran around. I wondered if I should leave the ring and let him play on his own, but I got a little nervous right then about getting to the gate. If he was coming toward me, would he stop? I didn't know. I did decide to hold the two ends of the lead rope together and swing the loop toward him if he came too close, but when I did that, I felt like I was chasing him away.

He went around me to the left.

I stepped backward and to the right, and he turned inward, the way he was supposed to, and headed to the right, but he bucked and squealed and kicked up. I saw his back hoof. It was nowhere near me, but it looked like it was pointed at me.

When my father's brother John was fifteen, back in Oklahoma (Daddy would have been twelve), he went to put one of the mules they had out in the corral with the other mule and the four horses. He opened the gate, led the mule through, and took off the halter. The mule leapt forward, twisted, and kicked out. He kicked Uncle John right in the side of the head, above his ear. Uncle John fell down, and Uncle Luke found him there sometime later, when Grandma sent him out to see why John hadn't come in for supper. He was already dead. They figured out what happened by the bruise above his ear.

When a horse kicks, you don't ever say that he or she meant to get you. It's your job to know that a horse (or a mule) can always kick and to stay out of the way. Some people would say that that is your number 1 job—you never approach a horse from behind, especially the first time; you always keep your hand on him when you go around his hind end, and you stay right up by him, because when you are right next to him, he can't land one on you. You stand to one side when you pick up his back feet or brush him back there or comb his tail. When you are riding in a line of horses, you stay back and keep your eye on the horse in front of you for any sort of threatening gesture. I knew about kicking as well as I knew anything. I knew that maybe the mistake Uncle John made was that he didn't walk his mule through the gate and turn him so that they were facing each other, and then take off the halter. I knew *all of this*, but I couldn't help thinking that after what I had done for Jack, and what I had thought of him, he still wouldn't mind kicking me if he was mad at me. I flicked the rope at him again, and he ran around the arena, squealing and bucking. I stood there.

I was not doing what Jem Jarrow would have done, which was to make Jack do stuff, at least change directions lots of times and stay back from me until he was a little worn out. I had done that with Jack over and over and never minded it because I enjoyed watching him. I realized I had better do that now, and so I did, flagging him on with the loop of rope, stepping back so he would turn, flagging him back the other way, and then, after he had gone a few strides, doing something sudden (even shouting "Boo!") so that he would jump and get the tension out of his back, the way I had done with Rally (though I kept thinking of Rally as Ornery George). And it was true that the more things I had Jack do, the more I enjoyed watching him, and the less I thought about whether he really loved me or not. Daddy hated it when anyone talked about horses loving someone. As far as he was concerned, horses were all about the carrot and the stick—they were good for carrots and stopped being bad if you hit them with a stick. And asking whether horses "loved" you was almost blasphemous—love comes from God, and horses, as far as we can tell, don't know anything about God.

Jack was trotting to the left. He had calmed down some, and his steps were brisk but even. He arched his neck and turned his head a little toward me, and I stepped back so he would turn inward and go the other direction. His neck arched a little more, and his tail lifted, and then he did turn inward, but he did not go the other direction. He trotted toward me, and then, when he was right in front of me, he reared slowly upward, looking me in the face. He stood there. Then he came down and turned to the right and trotted away. I was surprised.

Then I realized that Daddy had come home while we were working and was standing outside the pen, looking. He said, "That colt is getting bossy."

I said, "He does feel peppy today."

"Has he ever done that before?"

"What?"

"You know what, missy."

"No."

"He was testing you."

"By rearing?"

"Of course."

By now, Jack was standing by the rail, quiet but looking at me.

Daddy added, "He could have hurt you."

"He didn't."

"Sheer luck."

"I don't think so."

Daddy took a deep breath. Now he was Being Patient. "Why don't you think so?"

"Because when he reared up, he looked at me, and when he looked at me, he curled his front legs back. He did. I saw him."

But I knew that Daddy was right, too, and that I had better get Jack to do things, plenty of things, because for the last half hour, I had been thinking about whether he loved me or not, not about whether he was behaving himself, and even though he curled his forelegs back and did not touch me with them, the way he touched the geldings, he really should not have reared up at me in the first place. I went to the side of the pen where we kept whips and found the flag, which was a whip with a piece of cloth tied to it.

I went back to the center of the pen.

Daddy was still standing there, but he didn't say anything, the way the teachers don't say anything when you are taking a test. I flicked the flag toward Jack, who was looking pretty hard at me, anyway, and he jumped and then trotted to the right. I flagged him on so that he would go a little faster, and then, when he kicked out, I flagged him on again. He bucked. I flagged him on again. Only when he was trotting nicely, around the outside of the pen, and looked where he was going in a businesslike manner did I lower the flag and let him slow down. He slowed down. But before he stopped, I flagged him on again. The thing is, he has to get the feeling that when he does something that he wants to do, it is you who is letting him do that. If he does something he wants to do that you don't want him to do, then you have to keep making him do that until he doesn't want to do it anymore. Or, as Daddy might say, the wages of sin is that you have to keep sinning until they let you stop, at least if you are a colt. I stepped back. He turned toward me, looking at me. I stepped back again. He stepped toward me and lowered his head. So I went up and petted him a couple of times on the nose. Then I stepped back and waved the flag so he would trot to the right. This time, he trotted nicely.

Daddy said, "That's better."

Jack turned in toward me again, lowered his head again. I stepped up to him, facing him, and lifted both my hands and waved my forefingers at him. He dropped his head just a little more and took a step backward. He was ready to consider further suggestions. I snapped the lead rope back onto his halter and then asked him to step over to the right and then to the left. He did what he was asked. Then I walked the lead rope around behind him and placed myself on his other side and pulled, just a little. He turned his head, turned it more, turned it more, until he was practically bent in two, and then he stepped under and turned his body all the way around until he was looking at me. I did this again, and then wrapped him the other direction, so that he had to turn all the way around. Then I petted him. His head was down and his ears were flopped. He was a good boy at last. I scratched him lightly all along the roots of his feathery mane, and he leaned into the scratching just a little bit. He gave a groan.

Daddy said, "You do a good job with him, but it's a good thing we gelded him."

I nodded.

"Well, I've got work to do. You want to ride Effie first or Happy?"

I chose Happy. He got on Lincoln. Ten minutes later, we were climbing the big hill behind the gelding pasture, toward the Jordan ranch. What with the heat and then everything else we were doing, I hadn't been up the hill in two weeks. Happy was a small mare, muscular and strong. She climbed the hill as if she had been waiting just to do that very thing for days. Lincoln had a harder time. But the weather was good, and about halfway up there was a breeze. It smelled sweet.

The surprise was the calves, six of them with their moms, up under the oak trees. They had long, dangly ears and triangular heads. Their skin hung in wrinkled folds, and they were blue, the color of smoke. I had seen plenty of calves over the years, both brown Herefords with white faces and black Angus. Calves were always cute. But these Brahmas were really cute. The one nearest the fence had a dark-colored crown on his head and a tuft the same dark color on the end of his tail. While we were watching, he started nursing the cow. I could see that she had a big hump where the withers would be on a horse, and he had a hump, too, though tiny. Herefords and Angus are flat across the top, head to tail. Brahmas are kind of surprising-looking if you aren't used to them. The cows and calves were noisy—there was a lot of mooing.

We walked the horses along the fence and tried to get a look at all of the calves. Two were lying down, but the four that were standing had big knees and a fold of skin that dangled between their front legs. One of them was much more speckled with dark dots than the others—almost as if a drift of soot had fallen on him. The calves looked at us as we rode by, but it seemed like the cows couldn't be bothered with something as unimportant as a couple of horses. Happy was interested in the cows, though. As we walked along, she stared at them, her ears pricked. She was much more interested than Lincoln. I remembered what Jem Jarrow said, and thought that Happy really, really wanted to play.

Daddy said, "Good cattle for a dry area, and these look healthy enough, even the calves. I'd stick with Herefords, though, out here in California. Best flavor."

One of the calves watched us as we made our way along the fence and then suddenly mooed at us. Happy flicked her ears. The calf mooed again, and Happy whinnied. I laughed.

"I think she's saying, 'Let's have some fun!'" said Daddy.

"You never see this kind at the rodeo," I said.

"Too fast," said Daddy. "Brahmas can run when they want to. Jump, too."

"I love the color."

"These are beauties, no doubt about it," said Daddy. "I'll be interested in the bull when they turn him out in a couple of months. I haven't seen him yet."

We turned and began to make our way down the hill. I let

74

Happy pick her own trail—she was good at it and went diago-nally, first to the left and then to the right. She moved right along. Lincoln wasn't as good at it, and Daddy had to sit back with his heels way down, reminding Lincoln how to shift his weight backward. I never saw a horse tumble down a hill-side, but every so often I was surprised when one didn't. That was the way it was with Lincoln.

We could see our ranch from above—the house, the barn, the pen, the arena, and part of the gelding pasture, and most of the mare pasture. The valley was golden and rolling, and Mom's flowers looked bright against the broad expanse of grass. There was something else, too: off to the left, sitting on the hillside—that dog. We hadn't seen him in maybe a week, and I had sort of forgotten him, thinking he had moved on or something like that. He was sitting up straight, his back legs square and his front paws together, ears up. Every moment or two, he lifted his muzzle and sniffed the wind. He also watched us. But he didn't move. Daddy said, "Looks like he thinks he owns the place, doesn't he?"

We walked on down the hill. When we were about halfway down, the dog got to his feet and walked after us, step by step, watching what we did. When we got to the barn and dis-mounted, the dog stopped where he was, maybe a third of the way up the hill on the other side of the gelding pasture, and sat down again. He still looked like he owned the place. Daddy watched him for a long moment before walking Lincoln over to the gelding pasture and putting him away, but he didn't say anything.

By the time we were on our last horses of the day, Sprinkles and Sunshine, the dog was gone.

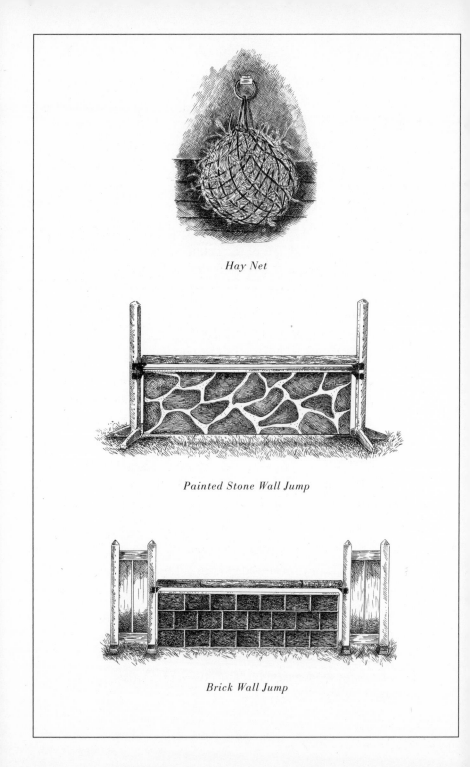

Hay Net

Painted Stone Wall Jump

Brick Wall Jump

Chapter 6

I GUESS I THOUGHT THAT NO TIME WOULD HAVE GONE BY SINCE I showed Gallant Man in his pony classes in the spring, and nothing would have changed, including me, because I was actually amazed when I tried on my show clothes the night before we were to take Black George over to the show and discovered that the sleeves of my jacket were too short, and Mom had to stand in front of where I was sitting in a chair and pull and pull on the bottoms of my jodhpurs to get them down over the tops of my jodhpur boots. As for the waist snap, well, we didn't even try to make that stick together—I just put a safety pin at the top of the zipper and covered the whole thing with a belt. At least my hard hat fit, but I knew that, because I had worn it when I schooled Black George, and my boots fit, because they were new. But I could feel the fronts of them if I spread my toes—they weren't going to fit for long. When I moved around in the front seat of the truck as we were driving Black George over there, I could feel my shirt popping out in back, too. I felt truly stupid.

And, of course, the first person I saw when I got there was Sophia Rosebury. Sophia Rosebury was exactly my age, and she was a big star around that barn—her instructor was not Miss Slater but Colonel Hawkins himself. Colonel Hawkins ran the whole barn (Miss Slater worked for him), and he had been on an Olympic team sometime, though I could never remember which team or when.

Sophia Rosebury was built like a pencil—maybe an inch or two taller than I was and about half as big around. She wore very large braces on her teeth—bigger than any I had seen in school—and she had blond braids down to the middle of her back. She was not what Stella would have called "so attractive!" but Sophia Rosebury was a good rider—anyone could see that—and her horses were nice, though not especially nicer than Gallant Man and Black George. What Sophia Rosebury had was perfect equipment. Her saddle was still tan—almost new, but rosy and supple. Her bridle matched her saddle. Her jacket fit as though it had been made for her, and she wore high boots—shining black ones. Nothing Sophia Rosebury was wearing was poking out where it shouldn't be. Her stock sat neatly underneath her jacket collar; her breeches went smoothly into the tops of her high boots. Her sleeves met her gloves and covered their edges. The same could not be said about me.

We were at the show grounds for about fifteen minutes

before Daddy managed to find Miss Slater—long enough for me to unload Black George and tie him to the trailer and watch Sophia Rosebury be given a leg up onto her perfectly cleaned and braided horse, then have her boots wiped by someone who must have been the groom. When she was absolutely clean in every possible way, Colonel Hawkins looked her over, and they walked toward the warm-up ring.

When Miss Slater saw me, I could see that she agreed with my feelings about my outfit, because she took one look at me and said, "Oh dear."

I looked down. The cuffs of my jodhpurs had ridden up and were about halfway up my legs. Well, that's what it seemed like. They were not that short, but they were too short.

Black George looked good, though. Between us, Daddy, Mom, and I had spent all day the day before trimming him and bathing him and combing out his tail hair by hair. His tail, in fact, looked spectacular—black and shiny and almost brushing the ground, so full at the bottom that it seemed to float. And, of course, the saddle and bridle were clean. Daddy knew how to get things clean.

Miss Slater looked at her watch, then she said, "We have twenty minutes before we have to warm up. Abby, come with me. I'll take you to the storeroom."

I followed her into the regular barn, where she crossed the courtyard to a door without a window, painted green with white trim. She pulled out a bunch of keys and unlocked the door. Inside it was dark. She pulled the string on an overhead light. The shelves were stacked with all sorts of things—not only clothes but bits and spurs and pieces of tack. She said,

"Some of these things have been here since the twenties. Someone should write an article." She waved her hand. "A few of those bits are positively terrifying." She picked up a roweled spur that looked like six nails set into a roller. "Not to mention this. There's only one of these, though. It's pure silver, so we haven't thrown it out."

She rummaged on one of the shelves and pulled out a pair of jodhpurs, then held them up to my waist. They were a little long, but she said, "These will do for now." Then she said, "Actually, dear, you are too old for jodhpurs. I should have realized that. You need to be wearing breeches and tall boots."

I said, "Daddy will not want to buy those. Are they, like, twenty dollars?"

"They are, like, forty-five dollars, new. But we can find some used ones, I'm sure."

If Sophia Rosebury had ever worn anything used, well.

Miss Slater handed me the jodhpurs and went to the door to keep watch while I changed. They fit okay. They were long enough, and the waistband buttoned. So what if they were extra-wide in the leg. After I put my boots back on, Miss Slater said, "Well, those are right out of the Second World War. But *very* durable goods. Pure wool twill."

I could tell that when we got outside. But they were loose and comfortable. Then she looked at my sleeves and pulled my shirt out a little more. She said, "It's always proper to show a little cuff. No one minds that."

Back at the trailer, Daddy had Black George saddled up, his mane combed again. As soon as I got on, Black George started tossing his head toward the arenas. At first, I thought there was something wrong with him, but then I realized that he just wanted to get going, and he was letting me know where to.

I decided that my main goal was to learn my courses and to not make any mistakes. I knew Black George would jump clean if I got him to the jumps.

We were going in low hunter classes—nothing big or recognized—since this was Black George's first show. And we were only signed up for two that day, a two-foot, nine-inch and a three-foot class.

The warm-up arena was crowded, but I remembered right-hand to right-hand when I was passing the others, and there weren't any near collisions or dirty looks. I noticed that Sophia Rosebury was in my class. She went second—they shined her up just before she went into the ring. I couldn't help watching her, and she did fine. Her gray mare (I heard them say "she" when they were talking about the horse) seemed to know her job. She pricked her ears before every fence and pulled up her knees. She was soothing to watch.

The first course was as simple as could be—walk in, do a right-hand circle, then gallop down one side, two jumps, and back up the other, two jumps. Then take the first jump again, cross the center, take the third jump going the other way, go around to the left, take the second jump backward, cross the center again, over the fourth jump backward—a circuit followed by a figure eight. There were two simple verticals of natural poles, one white chicken coop, and a solid jump painted to look like a stone wall. Black George did everything perfectly, including change leads when he was supposed to. I had no idea how they would judge him, but his first horse-show round was a success.

Not everyone made it look so easy. There was a woman after me on a brown horse with two white socks. She cantered down to the stone wall, and the horse paused and then jumped it almost from a standstill. At the next vertical, he just stopped and dropped his head. She rolled over his neck and somersaulted, then landed on her back. I must have gone "Ha!" because it shocked me, but then she sat up and brushed herself off. A woman sitting on the railing of the warm-up near where I was walking said to her friend, "That happens to her all the time. I don't know why she keeps at it."

The woman who fell off now stood up, and took the reins of her horse and led him out of the arena. I wished I hadn't seen it.

Sophia Rosebury went again, this time on a nice chestnut. This horse was as good-looking as the mare, but a different type—more elegant and sensitive. He was actually very beautiful, the sort of horse you couldn't stop staring at. I patted Black George, who was a handsome boy and always good, but this horse made him look like just a horse.

As they galloped around, their rhythm made me sort of forget where I was—jump gallop jump gallop jump gallop, and now they were coming to the coop, and two strides in front of it, as easy as you please, the chestnut horse ducked out to the right, almost out from under Sophia, who barely managed to sit up and halt him. Then she turned him back so that he was facing the fence, and she used her whip to smack him, once, twice, three times with her right hand while holding the reins tightly with her left. Then she turned a circle and came back to the jump. He jumped it, though a little awkwardly, then went on, completing the course. It took him until the last jump to re-gain his rhythm. The look on Sophia's face when she came out of the ring was halfway between crying and raging.

Colonel Hawkins stepped up to her with his mouth open, like he was going to say something, but before he could, she threw him the reins and jumped off. And I mean she jumped off—she did not dismount, where you put your hand on the horse's neck, lean forward, bring your right leg over the back of the horse, pause a second, and then drop to the ground. She was sitting there. Her right leg came over the horse's neck; she launched herself and landed. She said, "I hate this horse!"

"Did he spook? It looked like he—"

"There was nothing to spook at!"

"Shadows on the—"

I could see Daddy ten feet away, where he was eating his hot dog. His ears were as big as plates. I thought to myself, "Do not say anything to these people. Do not offer to take this horse off their hands."

"It's always something with him!" exclaimed Sophia. And she stomped off.

Ten minutes later, she came back to get her ribbon for her round with the gray mare—red. She looked normal again. Black George got a ribbon, too—white for fourth. If you'd asked me how the judge could see a difference between first, second, third, and fourth, I could not have told you. Everyone jumped nicely, went clean, and got their lead changes. But everyone was completely different, too—bay, gray, bay, almost black. Well, figuring it out wasn't my problem.

* * *

83

The second course was higher and a little harder. They brought in a fifth jump, a brush, and placed it at the end of the ring, making it part of the course. Then they turned the first jump and the third jump on a diagonal and brought them closer together, so they made an in-and-out. Then they added another set of natural-colored poles a few feet down from where the third jump had been. We were to trot in, go down to the far end of the arena, jump those poles, then turn over the in-and-out and go out and around over the new brush fence, then down the far side and up the near side—a circuit. To get to the last jump, you had to gallop between the two halves of the in-and-out and jump number 6, the brick wall again. Then you had to make a nice circle, come down to the walk, and leave the arena on a loose rein, "With a smile on your face," said Miss Slater when we were walking the course.

The good thing about the course was that when you had to turn a different direction, the jump you were turning from was the same sort of jump you were turning toward, so you could keep track of things that way. I stood in the middle of the arena with my fingers in front of my face and walked myself over all of the jumps. Then I did something else—I went backward, starting with jump number 8: 7 to 8; 6 to 7 to 8; 5 to 6 to 7 to 8. I thought this could either be a really dumb idea or a brilliant way to keep it in my mind. We would see.

Black George and I warmed up and went fourth. I did what Miss Slater said, took my time. We walked to the far end of the arena. We picked up a canter. We got the rhythm. We finished our circle. We went to the first jump. I could feel his hooves hitting the dirt beneath me, da-da-dum, da-da-dum, and then we were over the first jump and headed for the in-and-out. Up. Up. Around to the brush. His ears pricked. He folded his back underneath me. His forefeet touched the ground, and we were off down the long side, da-da-dum, da-da-dum. We jumped. We jumped again. And then—

And then I didn't know where to go. I could feel this ignorance shoot through me, but at the same time, I could also feel Black George keep going. Oh. Yeah. Down the second side, then around through the in-and-out and back over the wall. It would have been a dumb mistake, but we didn't make it. Thanks to Black George.

Miss Slater and Daddy were clapping when I came out of the ring. I didn't say anything. I gave Black George some extra pats, and then, when I got off, I kissed him on the cheek. Smarter than I was, again. I walked him around and took him back to the trailer. I could see Daddy and Miss Slater standing by the rail and talking a blue streak, as Mom would say. But I was tired and ready to go home. Riding your own horse at the show was much more exhausting than riding another person's horse, though I didn't know why. And anyway, it was still morning—they were still serving breakfast at the food tent. I had four horses to ride in the afternoon. After untacking Black George and walking him around for fifteen minutes, giving him a few drinks (though the weather wasn't hot), I tied him to the trailer and started brushing him down. He waved his tail back and forth and ate hay from his hay net. I yawned about ten times.

Then I saw Daddy trotting toward me from the direction of the ring, and in his hand he was carrying a blue ribbon.

I woke up right then. He said, "Well, Abby, I thought you were just about perfect that time around, and I guess the judge thought so, too." He leaned down and squeezed me around the shoulders.

"It was Black George who was just about perfect. I forgot where to go, and he remembered."

"At the far end, there?"

I nodded.

"Momentum was on his side. But I saw you turn your head."

"I don't know what to do about it."

"Keep trying is all. Pray, too." Then he kissed me on the top of my head, and we started picking up buckets and brushes and things.

And here came Miss Slater. She had a big grin on her face. First she patted Black George on the neck and said, "What a good, good boy!" Then she grabbed my shoulders and gave me a kiss on each cheek and said, "Abby, you are a first-class rider, no two ways about that!" And then she put her hand on Daddy's arm and looked him in the eye. She said, "You'll be back tomorrow, right? For the second class in the division and the hack class?"

Daddy was already shaking his head, but he hadn't spoken yet. Miss Slater didn't give him a chance to speak. She said, "People are already talking about him! I heard them. Arthur Killington asked the colonel who this horse was, and Letitia Merton was eavesdropping. His form is perfect, his rhythm is perfect."

Daddy said, "Well, maybe so, but we can't—"

"There was nobody like him in the class. He did fine in the

other class, over smaller jumps, but people saw in this class that his form is only going to improve as the jumps get bigger. And we *know* that's true, from the other day."

"Sunday is a bad day—"

"Sunday is the biggest day at a horse show!"

"Yes, but—"

"I, personally, will pay the entry fees! This horse has to be shown off, Mr. Lovitt. Believe me. There's—"

"We go to—"

"—thousands of dollars in it."

Now we were all quiet. Struck dumb, I guess. Daddy took off his hat and scratched his head.

"If you are going to go to church, that's fine. The classes are scheduled for the late morning. You can go to early Mass and come back out from there. I'll stick him in the barn, and you won't have to pay for a show stall."

That word *Mass* rang out like a blaring horn. Daddy took a deep breath and said, "We are not Catholics, Miss S—"

"Oh! Goodness! Sorry! I assumed if you *had* to go to . . ."

Now we were back at the silent part. I untied the hay net from the side of the trailer and carried it around to the back, then stepped inside the trailer and hung it up where Black George could eat from it while we were going home. Then I peeked through the slats of the trailer. Daddy and Miss Slater had walked away, and now they walked back. She was saying, "At least don't decide right this minute. Let the horse stay the night in case you change your mind. Think about it a little more. I just have a feeling that if certain people around here have a chance to see him tomorrow, it could be very important."

Daddy opened his mouth. Miss Slater reached up and untied Black George. Now she had the rope in both hands, just smiling and nodding. She was good. She was really good. Before Daddy had a chance to even answer, she said, "Oh, thank you, Mr. Lovitt. You will really be glad. . . ." Then she said, "There are people around here who do things purely on impulse, though they call it instinct. It's not a wise way to buy a horse, but when you are very successful at, let's say, trading stocks and bonds, then . . ." She gave a little shrug.

I came out of the trailer. She turned to me and said, "You did so well today, Abby. I am really proud of you." And she walked off with our horse.

Daddy stood there for a minute, looked after her, then he put his hands on his hips and said, "Well, no use taking the trailer home. We'll park it over there in the parking lot and then get it tomorrow when we come back."

He didn't say Monday. I didn't know what that meant.

We were home in time for lunch. We had tuna salad sandwiches and told Mom about the show. She knew better than to ask where the horse and the trailer were for the time being, and I knew better than to stay in the house after I was finished with my lunch. I changed into jeans and western boots and went out to the mare pasture, where I got out Happy and Sprinkles, who liked being together. I tacked up Happy and found a lead rope for Sprinkles, which I attached to her halter and threw over her back. Then, once I was on Happy, I could just grab the lead rope, and Sprinkles would walk along beside us, and both mares would enjoy each other's company. We would go down to the crick and see how the water level was.

But it didn't matter about me staying out of the house all afternoon, riding my horses and playing with Jack; they didn't actually talk about what we were going to do the next day until after I went up to do my homework. Or after they thought I'd gone up to do my homework. I was doing my French sentences, but I was sitting at the top of the stairs while I did them, not quite hiding but not sticking my legs out into the light or burping out loud, either.

Mom said, "Have you made up your mind?"

Daddy said, "Tomorrow is the Lord's day. We have plenty to do without adding in some horse show."

Silence.

Mom said, "Then you'll pick up the horse Monday?"

Daddy said, "I ought to pick him up tomorrow, at least. I can do it late."

"We'll go to church in the truck, then?"

"We can."

Silence. Rustle of a page turning.

Mom said, "Did she really say thousands of dollars?"

"Yes."

"Not hundreds? I'm surprised that it would be thousands."

"That's what she said. Of course she's exaggerating."

After a moment, Mom said, "No doubt."

"Though I asked her . . . Well, there was a gray mare in the first class. Nice mare. Got second over Black George. Came from Virginia, and they paid eleven thousand dollars for that one. They paid six thousand dollars for a chestnut gelding, nicer conformation and movement, but a bit of a rogue, I thought."

"Eleven thousand dollars?"

"Well," said Daddy, "that's Virginia dollars. Maybe they aren't worth as much."

They laughed.

Mom said, "I'm sorry I didn't go. I would have liked to see them."

"The eleven thousand–dollar mare?"

"No, Abby and Black George."

"Is it prideful of me to say that they looked better to me than the gray mare and her rider?"

"No, not if they really did. You have to be able to judge. The Lord doesn't ask us to be blind to our virtues, if we can make use of them."

Pause. Sound of a kiss. My toes curled.

Mom said, "Thousands of dollars?"

"Well, if he wins. If he's champion. That's not a sure thing."

"So, all the championships are going to be decided on Sunday?"

"That seems to be how it works."

Creaking of the couch.

"What if someone else rides the horse?"

Daddy said, "I don't know who that would be. Maybe by the spring we can figure something out. This is the last big horse show of the year."

Long pause.

Daddy said, "People are up from Los Angeles. Down from Woodside. Big show."

"I thought there was one more show."

"Much smaller. More local."

Now there was a long pause and some low muttering, as if

Daddy were reading aloud from the Scriptures. Then he said, "I think a case could be made that the prohibition against working on the Sabbath might not apply to this. I mean, to Abby."

"How would it not apply?"

"She's a child. He's a horse. Are they working?"

Mom said, "Yes."

"You're right. Of course. Best forget it. I'll call Miss Slater in the morning."

"Good."

I sighed. That, I saw, was that.

Il lui jette la balle. I wrote, "He threw him the ball."

Jacques jette la balle à Jules. I wrote, "Jack threw the ball to Julius."

Elle lui jette la balle. "She threw him the ball."

Monique lui jette la balle. I wrote, "Monica to him threw the ball," then erased that and wrote, "Monica threw him the ball."

Dad said, "If we got three thousand for the horse, our tithe would be three hundred dollars. If we got eleven thousand for the horse, our tithe would be eleven hundred dollars."

"If we got eleven thousand for the horse, we could give twenty percent, simply out of gratitude."

"Gratitude for what?"

Pause, then, "Well, for the opportunity that's being afforded us by the coming of the horse. We didn't ask for such a horse. We didn't *seek* such a horse. The horse came to us."

Daddy said, "You mean, maybe the horse is a gift that we should not have doubt of."

"Maybe the true destiny of an animal that is given to you is to reach his highest purpose, and twenty percent of eleven thousand dollars going to the mission fields is his highest purpose. So certainly this could be working for the Lord on Sunday. There couldn't be anything wrong with that."

"Maybe. I don't know how to tell."

"Why do you choose these particular horses? Because they have a higher purpose. Who are we to say that what is happening to Black George isn't God's will?"

"The blue ribbon is a sign. There's one way to decide." A book—Daddy's Bible—closing.

"That's a good idea."

Pause. I set my French book down and put my arms around my knees. I wasn't sure what I wanted, either. But, of course, you were not to pray for or against any particular thing. I thought I could hear the Bible opening, but maybe not. Then I felt like I was going to sneeze, and I had to grab the point of my nose between my thumb and forefinger and wiggle it hard. It worked. The sneeze went away.

Daddy said, "Friend, go up higher. Then thou shalt have glory."

"Really?"

"Yes, but only after ye seek the lowest place. Truly, though, I opened to the page, and my eye fell on 'go up higher' first. I don't know. It's right in Luke 14:10."

"But then it says that he who is exalted shall be brought low. I don't know, either."

He closed the book. I could hear him.

The clock in the dining room struck eight times. I decided that this whole conversation made me sad, and I got up very quietly and went to my room. There I put my pajamas on. Even though it was a little cold, I opened the window and looked out at the geldings. The moon was almost full, and I could see them fairly well. Lester, who was light-colored, was taking a drink. Two dark ones, maybe Lincoln and Jefferson, were standing quietly together with their heads down. At first, I didn't see Jack, whose best friend was Black George, but then I did. He walked out from under a tree, swinging his head, then he stopped, pawed the ground, and laid down to roll. Over and back, over and back. I remembered a certain saying Uncle Luke once told me, that every time a horse goes all the way over, he's worth another thousand dollars. I smiled at that.

I closed the window and got into bed. I really wished that I had *Great Expectations* to bore me to sleep.

But I must have dropped off because it was only ten by my alarm clock (well, five after ten) when Mom sat down on my bed and woke me up. She turned on the light and said, "Honey, I'm sorry to wake you, but Daddy called Miss Slater, and she's going to be here at eight to give you a ride to the show. We're going to church, but we think you need to ride Black George. We'll come in the truck to pick you both up after church."

And that was how I ended up having the strangest Sunday of my life the next day.

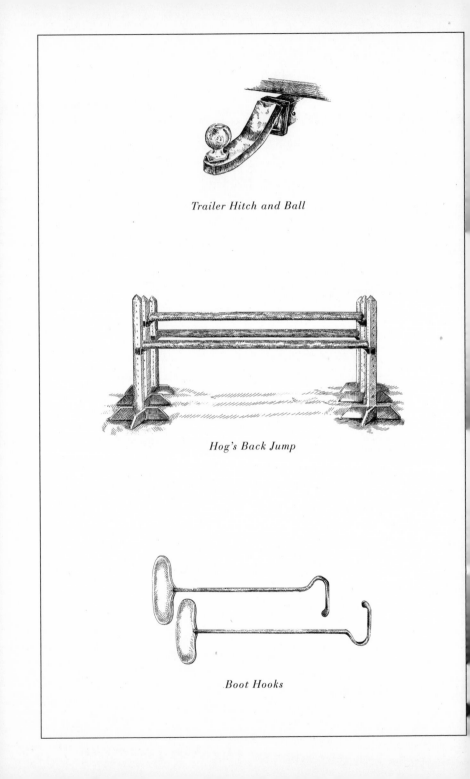

Trailer Hitch and Ball

Hog's Back Jump

Boot Hooks

Chapter 7

MISS SLATER WAS THE SORT OF PERSON WHO IS NEVER ON TIME if she can be a little early, so I heard her pull up at about ten to eight, after I had fed the horses but while I was still getting dressed. It was a cold, foggy morning. Mom had already ironed my shirt again and my stock. I put my raincoat on over everything, and I was in the front seat of Miss Slater's new Volkswagen and heading out the gate by eight. My saddle and bridle were in the trunk of the car, which was in front of us, not behind us. I had never been alone with Miss Slater without a horse before. She said, "Please put on your seat belt, Abby."

I put on my seat belt.

She said, "Your ranch is very neat. Lovely flowers."

"My mom does those."

"Does she ride?"

"She trail-rides two of the quieter horses."

"And the horses live out all the time?"

"Yes, ma'am."

"You don't have to call me ma'am. It makes me feel old. I'm only thirty-one."

That was younger than Mom. I gave her a quick glance, then said, "Okay."

"In fact, you can call me Jane."

"Okay."

"Anyway, I like it that your horses live out all the time. That's better, I think. But it's hard to persuade people that expensive horses won't simply do themselves in if given half a chance." She sighed.

Once we got to the main road, we stopped for her to get a cup of coffee. She turned to me and said, "Do you want a Coke?"

"It's breakfast time."

"Coke for breakfast is one of my favorite things." Then we laughed, but I didn't want a Coke for breakfast. I had a carton of milk. We drove on. The Volkswagen made a happy putting sort of noise, as if it really weren't a car, but it ran fine.

When we got to the stable, we went straight to the stall Black George had been put in the night before. It was perfectly clean already, with the straw mounded up along the walls, and Black George was brushed and gleaming. He came to the door of the stall and nickered to me. I stroked him down the face and neck, and Jane Slater gave me a cube of sugar, which I offered him. I said, "I don't think he minds this."

"Not for one night," said Jane. "But look at them all. They're bored sick, some of them. Weaving. Cribbing. Kicking the walls of the stall. Look in that one."

I looked over the door of a horse two stalls down. One whole side of the stall was dented and scraped. Jane said, "That mare runs her teeth back and forth over that spot four or five hours a day. Just bored to tears. But the owner won't let her go out for fear that she'll run around and hurt herself." She shook her head. "It's a shame."

Then she said, "But come with me. I found you something."

I gave Black George a last pat and we headed down the barn aisle, only to stop by Gallant Man's stall for a moment when he nickered and give him a piece of sugar and a pat. He looked cute and fat and whiter than he had been in the spring. Jane said, "I wish Melinda could come back, but there are a couple of little girls riding him. Beginners. He's happy."

I saw that I would be too big for him now.

She led me into the main tack room, which was next to the office. Over the back of a chair was a pair of canary breeches, and beside the chair was a pair of high boots, polished to an ebony shine. She said, "The breeches might be a little big, and the boots might be a little small. But try them on. We'll see."

She took a pair of boot hooks off the desk.

I took off my jodhpurs and boots and put on the breeches and buttoned the buttons down below my knees.

You don't need boot hooks with jodhpur boots or cowboy boots, but I knew how they worked—you hold the handles and slip the hooks into the flat little loops inside the tops of the boots, then you stick your foot in toe first and slide yourself down into the boot. If you can. And I could, with the right boot. It was a little tight, but I just pulled harder, and down it went. My right leg looked good. I had to admire it.

Then I slipped the hooks into the loops of the left boot and stuck my toe in, balancing on my right foot. My foot would go in only so far, and then there I was, half in, half out. I pulled and pulled on the hooks and pushed and pushed on my foot, but couldn't get my heel down below the ankle of the boot.

"Hmmm," said Jane, trying to help me by sitting down and shoving on the sole of the boot. The thing seemed stuck—not going on, not coming off. Jane said, "I guess your left foot is bigger than your right. Or Lily Grayson is built opposite to you. She has a horse here, but she's gone to college, and I know— Well, let's try something else."

I sat down in the chair and she pulled the boot off. Then she went over to the row of lockers and opened one. She took out a pair of stockings and handed me one. She said, "Take off your sock and pull this over the bottom of your breeches leg." We did that and tried the boot again. It slid on. But it was tight. I flexed my ankle. That was okay. But I knew I would have to make myself not think about how tight the boot was. We left my things in the locker and went out to get Black George. The boot. Was. Tight. I was limping by the time we got to his stall.

There was a man there, about my height, slender and wiry. He said, "Are ye ready, then, lass?" And Jane said, "Yes, thank you, Rodney." He turned to me and gave me a big grin, then he held out his hands and said, "Let's throw ye up there, lass." And he did. I put my knee in his hand, and he nearly launched me over Black George and onto the roof of the barn.

Jane said, "Abby, this is Rodney Lemon. He's been working for us for about a year. He's from England."

I said, "Nice to meet you, Mr. Lemon," and he gave a little bow, but with a big grin on his face, like he was making fun of everything, including himself. As we walked away, he smacked Black George on the haunch and said, "That's for a bit of luck, now!"

"He's a character," said Jane.

But he had done everything—cleaned the horse, cleaned the tack, pinned the number to the saddle pad, oiled Black George's hooves so they shone, combed the mane and the tail. As I rode along, I felt rather proud of how we looked, and then, of course, I had to hope that pride wouldn't goeth before the fall in this case.

As if she were reading my mind, Jane said, "Now, Abby, you are a lovely rider. I don't know where the natural talent ends and the years of experience begin. But the sort of lovely rider you are is very modest, if you know what I mean: you do your job and stay out of everyone's way. That's fine in your over-fences classes—you want the horse to seem as though he is taking care of everything in a hunter class. But in your hack class, where you're all together and going around the ring not jumping, you want to make sure that every time the judge looks at a horse, your horse is the one he sees. I wouldn't say this if you had a poorly trained horse, but you have a well-trained horse, nice-looking, with good conformation and movement. He is not flashy, though, and he doesn't have any white markings to draw the judge's eye. Therefore, my dear, put yourself out there where the judge can't miss you, okay?"

"Okay."

But first there was the jumping class. The course was once again fairly simple, a figure eight followed by a long loop across the center of an in-and-out followed by a chicken coop, and then a turn to the brush, around the first jump and across the center, over a jump set perpendicular to the others. I walked the course with my feet and then with my fingers, and then I jumped in the warm-up and did everything Jane told me, and then I was in the ring, and Black George was trotting, circling, cantering, and the next thing I knew, we were turning left down the long loop, right over the brush, then around the first jump and across the center, over some natural poles. I sat up, came to the trot, and left the arena with a smile.

It wasn't until I was back out in the warm-up arena that I felt my left leg throbbing inside the boot. I took my foot out of the stirrup and twisted it around and around, first to the outside, then to the inside. Jane came over. She was very pleased. She said, "That should be a winning ride. We'll see. Depends on how big a hangover the judge has this morning and whether he's seeing double or not." She grinned, then became very serious. She wasn't exactly the same person I had thought she was.

She watched the other rounds—there were eight after me. Three horses had refusals, which was very bad for a hunter, and one of those plus one other knocked rails down, which, according to Jane, wasn't good but wasn't terribly bad if the horse's form was good. Sophia Rosebury's gray mare had a good round. The lady who had fallen off the day before did not fall off this time, but her horse bucked twice, also not good for a hunter. A hunter was supposed to buzz around like a robot, so that you, the rider, could keep your mind on the fox or blow your horn for the hounds or something like that. I said, "Jane, have you ever gone foxhunting?"

"Oh, I grew up doing that, in Pennsylvania. Radnor Hunt. Twice a week when I could skip school. But then I moved out here."

"Can you hunt here?"

"If you want to hunt coyotes. But it's not the same when you've done the other. My favorite place to hunt is France. They hunt stags in the forests. I love Picardy. You go out into the forest all day, and then you eat ham and cheese omelets and drink brandy by the fire at night." She smiled. "I only did it once, but I can't wait to do it again. No jumping, but it's fun."

The last horse, a small bay, completed his round. I thought he had seven good jumps, but one was bad—he paused in front of the brush and leapt from almost a standstill. When they called us in for the ribbons, Sophia's mare was first and Black George was second. Jane said, "She was third in the class yesterday, did I tell you that? So you're ahead, but just. This hack class will tell the tale." She turned and put her hand on my stirrup and stared up at me. She said, "That's a very expensive mare, Abby, and Black George has her beat at this point. She's perfect in the hack class and often wins, but she has a bit of a Roman nose."

"What difference does that make?"

"The judge will *always* go for the pretty one, if all things are equal."

"Daddy says a pretty head is worth money."

"Sad to say, he's right. It's only English people who think a Roman nose is a sign of character in a horse."

The hack class was called, and the other horses began to

file into the ring. Jane sent me in right after Sophia and her mare, which I now knew was named Lorena, as in "The years creep slowly by, Lorena," one of Daddy's favorite non-hymns. I knew without Jane saying anything that my job was to stick with Lorena and get between her and the judge as often as I could without seeming rude or pushy. Sophia knew that, too. I could tell by the way she sometimes looked at me that even if the day before she might not have known my name or who in the world Black George was, now she did. I also knew that she could see that my sleeves were too short and my boots too tight and my breeches too big.

The announcer asked for a trot, and I lifted my chin and floated by her, sort of the way the Big Four floated by the rest of us in seventh grade, as if we weren't to be looked at. No, that was wrong. The real thing to do was to float by everyone the way the Goldman twins did—not feeling self-conscious at all, just going about your much more interesting life because it actually is much more interesting. I thought, Alexis Barbara Alexis Barbara, and passed two of the others, too, including the woman who always fell off. I could hear her talking: "Easy now. Easy now. Settle down!" Her horse did not look excited, though. We were asked to reverse. This time, I didn't pass Sophia and Lorena. I stayed two lengths behind them and matched them stride for stride. Only when we came to the end of the arena did I let Black George go to the inside and pass them. Sophia gave me a dirty look, which I *felt* but did not *see*.

Now we were told to canter. I sat down, lifted my inside hand. I felt Black George lighten up his shoulder and rise to the canter like a bird rising on a breath of air. It was delicious.

Frankly, it was so pleasant that I forgot for a moment about Sophia and winning and eleven thousand dollars, and just cantered to the end of the arena for fun. Then we were asked to hand-gallop. I got into my half seat, and Black George extended his stride. It occurred to me that the easiest thing to do right then would be just to keep going and jump right out of the arena.

But I didn't do that.

When I passed Jane, she was smiling.

Halt.

We halted.

Trot on.

We trotted on.

Reverse.

We reversed and then cantered again.

I guess it was about then that I realized that I had lost track of Sophia and Lorena completely and in fact was more or less off in my own little world.

Then the others were lining up, so we came down to the walk and turned across the center. In the row of horses and riders, I stood between the little bay and the falling-off lady. The announcer called my name and the ringmaster held up the blue ribbon, and I walked right up to him as if I had expected that very thing. I held out my hand. He put the blue ribbon in it. I was so excited without realizing it that I headed the wrong direction, and Jane had to wave to me to get me to come out of the arena.

Five minutes later, I had a little silver dish in my hand. It was very pretty, small, with six petals, like a flower, and writing—the name of the horse show and the word *Champion* written on it. The championship ribbon was larger than the regular ribbons, with a long blue streamer, a long red streamer, and a long yellow streamer. Jane hung it from Black George's browband, down the side of his face. He looked very elegant.

Jane was grinning, and as we walked by Colonel Hawkins, she looked him in the eye and said, "Congratulations!" in a high, singsong voice, but what she really meant was "Take that!" The colonel smiled at her—he was her boss, after all—but Sophia gave us a very dirty look.

Rodney met us at the gate with a rag in his hand. While we were walking back to the barn, he wiped Black George's mouth and face, then ran the rag down his neck. He said, "That all for the day, then, miss?"

"For now," said Jane.

For now? My ears should have pricked up, but they didn't. Half of me was still staring at those waving streamers in the championship ribbon, and half of me was starving. When we got back to the barn and I dismounted, though, I nearly fell down—my leg was numb from the boot.

Rodney caught me and stood me on my feet.

"Oh my goodness," said Jane. "That boot is killing you! Why didn't you say anything?" She led me over to the mounting block and sat me down, then started pulling off the boot. It wasn't easy, and once Rodney had put Black George in the stall, he had to help. It felt like they were pulling off my foot. They pressed on the toe, then pulled on the toe, then wobbled the heel, then pressed on the toes, then pulled on the heel. Rodney finally stood with his back to me, bending over and holding the heel. Then he said, "Put yer foot right on me arse, lass, and give me a push."

Jane said, "Rodney!" But she laughed.

I did what he told me, and he managed to pull the boot off. Then Jane slipped off the stocking, unbuttoned my breeches leg, and began to rub my calf. It started to tingle and then started to burn, and then Rodney started slapping the bottom of my foot and rubbing my ankle. First it felt normal, and then the muscle down the side of my leg started to hurt. Miss Slater said, "You need to walk around. Get the circulation moving! I'll go to the office and get your things." While she was doing this, Rodney got Black George out of the stall and took him over to the hose. There was something very nice about sitting on the mounting block and having someone else take care of the horse. I thought I could get used to that really quickly.

Jane came back with my jodhpur boots and the World War II twill jodhpurs, and I went into Black George's stall and changed. Then I walked around, as she had told me to do, until my leg was no longer throbbing, just aching a little bit. Then she said, "Abby, you must be starving," and took me to the food tent, where she bought me a cheeseburger and fries and that Coke that I had had in the back of my mind since breakfast. Mom and Daddy and I were not the kind of people who went to the food tent—we were the kind of people who packed along some sandwiches and fruit and drank from the drinking fountain—so sitting in the food tent with a juicy cheeseburger and some very crisp fries was fun. I said, "Thank you for everything, M— Jane, but I am a little afraid of getting used to this."

"You mean, getting to be like Sophia Rosebury. I know. That girl hasn't cleaned a stall in her life."

"Well, I didn't mean that, exactly, only that if I get used to this, then—" But at that moment I thought about my regular life, the life of the geldings and the mares and rubbing down Jack and having lessons from Jem Jarrow and riding down to the crick and up to the cows and calves, and I realized that this was fun, but a whole life of it wouldn't be. So I said, "You should come visit us sometime."

"Try it your way? I would like that. I could wear jeans instead of breeches and high boots all the time."

I nodded. Then I said, "Does Rodney ride?"

"Oh, my dear. Makes your hair stand on end. He'll ride anything. I think he was born riding chasers in Newmarket."

"Chasers?"

"Steeplechasers. They race over jumps."

"Like in *National Velvet*."

"Exactly. Did you like that book?"

"I liked the parts I understood. I couldn't picture some of it."

"Very English. Did you see the movie?"

I shook my head. "We don't see movies or have a TV."

"Well, the riding parts were filmed right around here. That was twenty years ago, but you can tell. The sunlight is not like England, that's for sure. Anyway, Rodney had a bad accident and lost his nerve a bit, so Colonel Hawkins got him over here to do something different."

"He seems nice."

"It's been two years and he still rides, but I don't know if he'll ever race over fences again. Anyway, here's a Rodney story. There's a lady who has a stud farm out in the valley. She breeds racehorses. She had a very tough two-year-old that they had not been able to break, and her farm manager happened to meet Rodney at a party. The two of them had had a lot to drink, and Rodney started to boast about how he could break anything, horses in England are a lot tougher than in California, et cetera. Then he woke up the next morning to a phone call taking him up on his boast—which he could not remember, in fact. But he got up and went out there.

"They had the colt in a stall. Rodney got on him in the stall, and at once, the colt leapt up and bashed Rodney's head into the ceiling. Fortunately, he had his hard hat on, but it sort of knocked him out and pushed the hard hat so far down on his head that he couldn't get it off. Then the horse leapt forward and rammed his own head into the front wall of the stall, and knocked himself out—he went to his knees and sort of reeled around, but he didn't fall over. A minute or so later, both Rodney and the horse came to, and Rodney was still sitting on the horse. After that, the horse was broke—Rodney stayed on, the horse was convinced, and he was good. Rodney has been a little more cautious since then, I must say."

I was impressed by this story—it reminded me of Uncle Luke. I said, "That lady should get to know Jem Jarrow."

"Who's that?"

"He helps us with the difficult horses. He lives on a ranch."

"Hmm." But I could see that she had lost interest already.

After we threw our paper plates into the trash can, Jane said, "What time do you expect your dad?"

"Church is over about four. Sometimes, if the singing is really good, they go to almost five." Suddenly, I hoped that the singing would not be really good today. It made me sad to miss it. Jane looked at me for a long moment, then said, "How many hours are you at church on Sunday?"

"About seven, including dinner. Dinner takes about two hours."

"I never heard of that before." She looked at me and then at her watch. We walked back to the stall in silence, and I did wonder what I was going to do for the rest of the afternoon. I guessed I would wander around, looking at the horse show. She said, "Want to go in another class?"

"Do I have to wear the boots?"

"Oh no. You are a real hero for wearing that boot. I had no idea. No. You can wear your own boots."

"What kind of class?"

"A jumping class, not a hunter class. Just to try it out. A more twisty course, and bigger, but some horses like it better because it's more interesting. Come on over here. I'll show you."

We went to a ring I had seen from afar but hadn't really looked at. It was bigger and had a few trees growing right in it. The jumps, I have to say, were more like the ones Daddy had set up for Black George at home—though no stuffed animals and no rows of books. But they were much more lively and interesting than the jumps I had been jumping, with different kinds of gates and brush, and several things set together. The other thing was that there were a lot of them in the ring. While we were standing there, a class began. The first rider was a man on a big bay. He walked into the ring and immediately started to trot. He made his circle and then, as far as I could tell, jumped every single jump from a different direction. And the course was longer—ten jumps rather than eight. The horse did not jump nicely at all—his head was up and his eye was rolling. He went fast and made tight turns. His tail waved this way and that, and even, over one jump, flipped upward. I couldn't tell if he liked it or not, but he did get around without a refusal or a knockdown. Afterward, the announcer announced that he had no penalties and he was within the time. Then the next person went, a woman on a nice paint horse. They had a knockdown, for four faults.

After they came out of the ring, I said, "I don't think I can do that."

"Oh, Abby!" exclaimed Jane. "But doesn't it look like fun?"

"If I could find the way around, it might be fun."

"Well, let's see what happens in the jump-off."

The jump-off, it turned out, was when the horses who had no faults and were within the time had to come in, one by one, and jump another, shorter round, this time against the clock. If I had thought that the first horse was going fast and rolling his eye the first time I saw him, then that was nothing compared to the way he went the second time. I didn't see how the rider could stay on, actually, the turns were so tight, but he crouched there with his legs clamped to the horse's sides and his arms and hands following every move of the horse's head and neck. Sometimes, it seemed as though the horse had only one or two strides to gather himself and jump the jump. But it was as if he were on springs. After the last jump, though, the rider sat up, let go of the rein, and walked out of the ring as if they had just been strolling about. That was what impressed me. Jane said, "That's Saint Joe. He's famous. He was on a Nations Cup team seven or eight years ago, but he's, what, nineteen or twenty now. He still likes it, though. A course like this is easy for him after what he used to do. He was always best in the jump-off. Sometimes a little careless in the first round."

I didn't know what to say.

The next horse in the jump-off had a knockdown, and the third horse was clean, but two and a half seconds slower. Jane said, "Should have gone to the next jump in front of that oxer, not around it. Distance is time in show jumping. Let's get Black George out."

I must have gone white, or something like that, because she laughed and said, "No, Abby. I changed my mind. I'm not going to enter you in a class like this. But I'm glad you saw it. This is where the glory is if you have a great jumper. I do so want to know what his pedigree is."

"We don't even know what his breed is."

"A mix, maybe, but lots of Thoroughbred, judging by his looks. Let's get him out for a bit. But no class."

I relaxed. The show went back to looking colorful and fun. When we started walking back to the barn, I said, "You should see our foal, Jack. He's— Well, the mare came to us pregnant, without Daddy knowing, and now they're saying she was stolen from a ranch in Texas, and that she was in foal to a horse named Jaipur. A private detective named Brandt has been sending us letters."

"Jaipur!" She stopped, turned, and looked at me. "He won the Belmont Stakes three years ago! And the Travers. He won the Travers by a nose, and it was in course record time!"

"But what if they take him back from us?"

As we turned down the aisle toward Black George's stall,

she stopped and looked at me, then put her hands on my shoulders and said, "All of these things are very hard to prove. Really, it is so hard to tell two horses apart, unless they have quite distinctive markings."

"Jack doesn't have any markings at all."

"Well, then, no doubt things will be fine. My goodness, Abby, you and your father are the most mysterious horse people I ever met! It's like you pull these wonderful rabbits out of your hat. You know no one, you drive an old truck and trailer, you live nowhere, and you've got horses people like Letitia Merton would kill to have. It's very fun and interesting!" She laughed and exclaimed again, "Jaipur!"

I could see Rodney, his cap pushed back on his head, sitting outside Black George's stall, cleaning tack. I was going to say more—I always liked to talk about Jack—but all of a sudden I didn't want to. "Goodness me," Jane said to herself. Rodney glanced at her.

Even though Black George was eating his hay, as soon as he saw us, he came to the door and put his head over and bumped me with his nose. There were some carrots in a bucket of water nearby, and I got one and fed it to him. He nodded his head while he ate it, which made me laugh. I thought I would like to get on him, if only to be around someone that I was real friends with. It seemed like days since I'd left home, even though it was only six or seven hours. I opened the stall door to get him out, but Rodney was there ahead of me. He said, "I'll do it, lass. You never know what trouble I'm going to get into if I don't keep busy." He laughed.

Jane said, "Isn't that the truth." But she was grinning. Once Black George was tacked up, I put on my hard hat and Rodney threw me into the saddle again—I was expecting the launch, so I landed a little better this time—and I followed Jane. We went past the hunter rings and the jumper ring we had visited, and came to a ring that looked like a show ring—all sorts of jumps were set up—but was not being used that day, though I had seen horses in it the day before.

Jane walked with me to the gate, then leaned her elbows on the fence while I went in. Black George seemed to be happy he was out of his stall—without me asking, he went up into a big, happy trot, and we trotted round the ring on a fairly loose rein, big strides, weaving in and out around the jumps. I picked up the reins and asked him to bend around those turns, and he did that, no problem. We trotted past the judge's stand (no judge) and a square bank, like the one on the outside course, only smaller. One side of the bank was about six inches higher than the other side—it was a neat little jump, and I thought it would be fun to try it. There were also coops and brushes and gates and oxers—both the kind where the back pole is higher than the front and the kind where the two poles are the same height. There was also a jump made of three poles, where the center pole was higher and the two side poles were lower. This was called a hogback, according to Jane. There was also a painted wall and something that looked like a quarter of a giant oil drum, called a "rolltop."

I trotted around and then cantered around, and then I stopped in front of Jane. She said, "I think Black George needs to have some fun."

This immediately made me think of that big ditch on the outside course, which had been, yes, fun in its scary way. My heart thumped, just once. But then, Jane pointed me down over a vertical made of natural poles, and it was just the same as usual, and my heart went back to its regular okeydoke sort of beat. There was no course to remember—down over the vertical, back up over the oxer, around and over the wall, then up and down the bank (which was just about the same height as jumping into and out of the crick at the bottom of the mare pasture), and so forth. Every so often, she went to the jumps and raised them a hole or two. Black George cantered everything, even the hogback, which seemed scary as we were heading toward it but not at all scary as we were going over it. Around and around.

The most fun was an in-and-out, two strides, made of a brush and then a gate. Jane raised the poles on top of these a couple of times. The key was to keep my heels down and stay still all the way to the in-and-out and then through it and away. My reins were fairly short, and so I could feel Black George gather himself under me, but the jump itself was smooth. I tried to remember all my rules—ride the path, not the jump; go to the center of the fence; look where you're going; don't lean into the turns. But mostly, I concentrated on looking up and keeping my heels down.

Finally, she waved me down to a walk. I couldn't tell how long we'd been jumping. In a way, it seemed like forever, and in a way, it seemed like no time at all. But even though I wasn't panting, and Black George wasn't panting, Jane was. She said, "My goodness, Abby. That horse makes these look easy as pie."

I said, "How high are they?"

I shouldn't have asked.

She pointed to the in-and-out. "The brush is four feet. The gate a little over."

My heart started thumping again. I wished she hadn't told me. I said, "You're kidding me, right? I don't think he's ever jumped over three feet before."

"Abby! He doesn't care how high it is. Some horses are like that. They're picky about how it looks or how they get to it, or how fast or slow they're going, but the height doesn't matter. You know that horse Jaipur?"

I nodded.

"His sire is a horse named Nasrullah. One of Nasrullah's first sons, oh goodness, twelve or thirteen years ago now, was a horse named Independence. He must not have been much of a racehorse, so he ended up a chaser. He won some big steeple-chases and made some track records. He would just jump anything, anything, and with joy. We don't know where that comes from, but once I had a horse who, if you put him out in a field with jumps, he would go jump them. Not to get out of the field or for any reason. Just because he liked it." She walked around with me as she said this.

I was still nervous. Four feet! I knew I would tell Daddy, and he would be impressed, and I knew I would tell Mom, and she would be upset. I was upset.

But I was excited, too. Just the way I had felt after the big water jump—the jump itself didn't scare me, but knowing that it was fifteen feet wide did. Jane went over and sat on the bank while I finished walking Black George around. I could see her staring at us, then she got out a little notebook and a pen and started writing things down.

When we were cooled out, I got off and led Black George

back to his stall. As we were walking along, she said, "Why did you name him Black George? That sounds like a pirate's name, and he's so sweet."

"We used to call all the horses George or Jewel, because Daddy didn't want us to get attached to them. So that was his name after we got him. Then I renamed all the others, but I still liked that name."

"I think you should name him Heart of Gold, because that's what he has."

Since I didn't have a watch, I had no idea what time it was, but as we were walking past the rings, I could see that the hunters were finished in our ring—the judge had left the judging stand—and the jumpers were getting their championship ribbons. At the show barns, trailers and trucks were pulled up, with their ramps down and their doors open. Various piles of tack trunks and other pieces of equipment were waiting to be loaded. I had no idea when Daddy would show up, but when we were almost to the barn, I saw him. There he was, over in the parking lot, hitching up the trailer. Mom was backing up the truck. I saw him raise his hand and the truck stopped, and he started to crank the trailer hitch down over the ball that stuck out from the back of the truck. I was really glad to see them. And Black George was, too. He whinnied loud and clear. Even though Daddy would not have called this love, I thought it was.

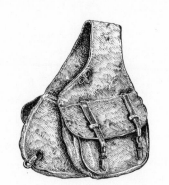

Saddle Bag

Mounting Block

Stall Door

Chapter 8

AFTER THEY HAD THE TRAILER HITCHED UP, IT TOOK DADDY and Mom a while to find a spot. Fortunately, we didn't have much to load—Black George didn't even have a blanket and had been using one of Jane's. But there was so much stuff lying around, and so many people and horses everywhere, that Rodney decided he had better bring the horse out. I carried my saddle and bridle. Even though I hadn't worn my raincoat since morning, I had it on now because it had started to drizzle. Rodney led Black George up to the back of the trailer, and then it was funny—he and Daddy did a little dance about who would load the horse. They looked each other right in the eye, and you could almost see their backs go up—it was like watching two dogs sizing each other up. Finally, Rodney said, "There ya go, guv'nor" as he patted Black George on the rump in a way that suggested that he was better friends with the horse than Daddy was.

When Mom and I piled into the cab, Daddy said, "Who was that fellow?"

I said, "He's a groom. He's from England."

Daddy humphed. Then I heard him mutter, "Doesn't act like a groom, if you ask me."

Mom had my ribbons and the little trophy in her lap. They had already congratulated me, but now she put her arm around me and said, "You did wonderfully well, Abby! Did you have a good time?"

I thought that the easiest thing to say was yes, and that's what I said. "No" and "Sort of" were both wrong, and if you were champion and you hadn't imagined being champion a mere two days before, then of course you had had a good time. "Almost"? "More than a good time"? "An unbelievably good time"? I didn't know what the right thing was. I said, "How was church?"

"Oh, they missed you." She kissed me on the cheek. "Brad missed you. Carlie had a hard time with those kids by herself." Watching the Greeley kids was a two-person job—that was certainly true.

Daddy said, "Those kids are old enough to settle down, that's my opinion."

I looked around Mom at him. He seemed in a bad mood. Mom lifted her eyebrows just a little. Then she said, "What's done is done, and I think it was worth it." She patted the ribbons and the trophy. "And not just because of the prizes. It seems like Abby got a lot of good experience, and both she and Black George will benefit from it."

After that, we were quiet.

I was tired. I dozed off on the way home.

It was dark when I woke up as we were turning into our road, past the mailbox. Maybe because I was sleeping, Daddy was the one who got out to open the gate, and I felt Mom (I was leaning on her shoulder) move over into the driver's seat to pull through. I yawned a couple of times. Mom stopped again, and then Daddy got in on my side after locking the gate. He yawned. She yawned. The yawns went around.

But we stopped yawning when we pulled up beside the barn and Daddy said, "What's that out there?" And then we sat up and really heard what we'd been hearing since we came through the gate—a lot of mooing and bawling. All the shapes resolved themselves in the twilight, and there they were, Mr. Jordan's cows and calves from up the hill, wandering around.

Mom said, "Uh-oh."

Dad said, "Must have broken through the fence."

Mom said, "What now?"

"Well, there's no place for them down here. They have to go back up the hill. You go in the house and call Jack Louis and I'll put Black George away." Jack Louis was the ranch manager.

I said, "What should I do?"

Daddy said, "Go change your clothes, honey, because my bet is that we are going to have to herd these animals back up the hill."

While I was changing my clothes, I didn't hear Mom talking

119

to anyone, so I figured that Jack Louis wasn't home. And when I got back outside, Daddy had put away Black George and gotten out Lester, Lincoln, and Happy. Both the geldings and the mares were standing by their gates, waiting for their hay, but when I went to get them some, Daddy said, "Better not. These cows are used to getting hay, and if they're hungry enough, they could break down our fences to get at the hay. Best just do this as fast as we can."

It was completely dark by the time we had the horses tacked up, though there was a three-quarter moon. Mom was being very quiet, and Daddy had to come over and tighten the cinch of her saddle. Then he kissed her on the forehead and said, "The Lord will provide."

She nodded.

We led the horses out of the barn. Daddy stepped onto Lester. Mom went to the mounting block and got on Lincoln. I climbed the gate of the gelding pasture. I did stop to pat Jack, who was snuffling my jeans pocket. As soon as I was in the saddle, I could feel that Happy was happy. Almost before I settled myself, she was trotting toward the place where the cows and calves had gathered in a group and were mooing and bawling. As soon as we got even a little close, though, the cows lifted their heads and started to walk around. Daddy raised his hand. I stopped, and behind me, Mom stopped.

We sat quietly while Daddy looked them all over, then counted them—six cows, six calves. Then he said, "Okay, the trick is to get them out from between the mare pasture and the gelding pasture and then up the hill to the left, around the gelding pasture, and back to where they broke through the fence."

He had some tools in his saddlebags, too, because he was going to have to fix the fence if he possibly could—that was four strands of barbed wire—"Should've been five, I can see that now," he said. "Now, Sarah, honey, you just walk along there, about ten feet from the fence of the gelding pasture, and, Abby, you walk along about ten or twelve feet from your mom. Just walk. I don't want them moving fast. I'm going to go through the mare pasture and be there when they come to the end of the fencing, and maybe they'll turn up the hill." He opened the small gate and went behind the mares, who were gathered by the fence, looking at the cows. There was another gate at the far end. He moved slowly; Sprinkles followed him for a few steps, then lost interest.

We did it. Lincoln was perfect for this. He didn't seem to care about the cows. Walking along was fine by him. Happy, though, was a little eager. If there were cows, then you were meant to chase them, according to Happy. Her ears were pricked and she was jigging underneath me, but she wasn't hard to handle. She seemed to know that Daddy and Lester were up to something—when they went into the mare pasture, she whinnied. Someone in the gelding pasture whinnied back to her. The cows stared at us—we could see their eyes and tongues shining in the moonlight—and they bawled and mooed, but they moved—all but one, and when she didn't move, Happy turned of her own accord and went toward her. The cow got going—she trotted over to the group and joined them. Her calf was right on her heels.

I couldn't see Daddy, but I could hear him canter toward the far end of the mare pasture. I was sure that the cows could hear him, too—cows are as smart as horses and have plenty of opinions. But right then, their opinion of Daddy was that he wasn't their business. Mom and I walked along. Mom started singing, softly, *"Ridin' ole Paint, leadin' ole Dan. I'm goin' to Montan' for to throw the houlihan."* I could tell she was feeling better. I said, "What's a houlihan?"

"Sweetie, I have no idea. *There's feed in the coolie, there's water in the draw. Their tails are all matted, their backs are all raw.* Not these, of course. These live in the lap of luxury."

"I love their ears."

"And they have beautiful eyes."

I said, "Loud, though."

We laughed.

We walked very slowly, but now I could see that the first cow had come to the end of the fencing. Of the mares, Effie and Sunshine had walked along with us, on the other side of the fence, just out of curiosity, I guess. And Jack, too, was trotting around, as if the cows were his business, like everything else. He tossed his head and kicked up, then stood and snorted at them, his tail lifted and his ears pricked. The cows didn't even give him a look. Then I saw Daddy and Lester, standing like a statue just past the far gate of the mare pasture, where the fence turned down toward the crick. We did not want the cows to go that direction. As the first cow stepped out from between the two lines of fencing, Daddy stepped forward, but only two paces. The cow turned to avoid him, and her calf followed. The second cow was right behind the first one. I saw her stop and stare at Daddy, giving a big moo, then the first cow stopped, too. Daddy moved one step in their direction, careful not to get at all in front of them. They stood still, and then Lester tossed his head and snorted, and the two cows bunched together and turned a little more. It was then that they saw something—freedom, maybe—up the hill, and they began to trot.

Because the grass was so golden and there were no trees on the hillside, it was much easier to see the cows and the calves as dark shadows against the pale background. We could see Daddy, too—he turned Lester and walked him back and forth in a semicircle, as if he were making a little wall all by himself that the cows could not pass through. But Mom and I on Lincoln and Happy just kept walking. It wasn't until all of the cows and their calves were out in the open that Daddy waved to us to pick it up, and then we trotted just fast enough to keep up with the cows but not fast enough to alarm them. Cow number 3 and cow number 4 turned, too—a little farther out into the hillside than the first two, but they did turn, and then they hurried to catch up with the first two.

Then, right then when I was remembering what a long day it had been, and thinking how strange it was to be out here on Happy in the night when I had been jumping Black George sometime earlier in the day, right then when Mom was starting another song, sort of under her breath and to herself—*"From this valley they say you are going"*—right then, the cows took off, and they were fast. Daddy took off after them, always trying to stay to the outside of them, and Happy took off, too, with her head stretched forward like a dog after a bone. She meant it— she was so fast that I had to grab the saddle horn to stay with her. Behind us, Lincoln was doing something, because Mom stopped singing and went "Oh!" but I didn't know what it was, because I was too busy trying to stick with Happy.

We galloped in a big arc up the hill, and the cows were tearing along in a curving bunch, Daddy and Lester just ahead of them, Daddy leaning forward in the saddle. He was good at this—I had forgotten how good. He had grown up herding cows, and it didn't matter that he didn't get much practice in California. He just did what he knew to do. At one point, the cows slowed down, and I thought they were going to stop—it was a steep hill—but they started bawling and running again, and Daddy kept pressing them from the side and Mom and I kept pressing them from behind. When I got a chance to look back at her, she was holding the saddle horn, but she was keeping up. In fact, one of the calves veered to the left, and Lincoln went after it, and Mom stuck right with him. We got most of the way up the hill.

I could see the broken place in the fence against the hillside, and for a moment, the cows were heading right for it. Then the curve of the group folded too far to the left, and just when I saw this, Daddy must have seen it, too, because he cut in front of me, between me and Mom and the cows, and galloped up the hill, pointing them toward the hole. It was easy to see what I needed to do—I needed to get up a little faster and keep everyone turning. The plan was that Mom would keep driving and Daddy and I would make a kind of two-person chute at the gate, and the cows and calves would go through it.

It worked fine until one of the calves ducked behind me and ran back down the hill. Since all the cows and all the calves were in a group, as far as we knew (they weren't our cows, and we didn't know them personally), it was impossible to say why the calf broke away. The oldest of these calves was about three weeks old, so normally he wouldn't want to leave his mother. I saw Daddy on the hill pull up Lester and stare after the calf, then take off his hat the way he did when he didn't know what to do. The rest of the animals were still in a bunch sort of heading toward the break in the fence. I was below Daddy on the hill, and just then he waved to me to keep doing what we were doing. Happy stared at those cows, and when the group bulged outward in our direction, she made a little jump toward them. The bulge disappeared. And then the group seemed to break up, and one of the cows burst out and ran down the hill. That would have been the calf's mom. At first, she didn't look like she knew where she was going, and she ran sort of toward Mom, but then she turned, saw the calf, and headed toward it. Mom and Lincoln stopped and then came on up the hill. Daddy got the others back into a bunch, but this part was a little scary.

The gap in the fence was fairly small, which was good for repairs but bad for getting the cows through—you didn't want the outside ones to either break down the fence or get turned back. We had to slow down but keep going, and try to thread the needle. I could tell by the way Daddy was working at this that he had decided to think about the stray cow and calf later and just concentrate on the group. Then I saw the first cow go through the hole in the fence, with her calf right on her heels. Daddy and I closed in on them, or rather, Lester and Happy started being more firm in their instructions, and moving toward the cows with their ears pricked and their attitude very intent. At one point, one of the calves must have brushed against some wire, because it jumped away from the group and bawled, but Lester went for it and pushed it back into the group. Pretty soon more than half of the group—maybe five or six animals—were through the hole.

Then we heard Mom say, "Wow!"

Mom was still behind us, fifty feet down the hillside and coming up, but she had stopped and now waved down the hillside. Daddy was working the last of the cows, but I looked where she was pointing. That dog was running up the hill, straight for the calf and the cow. Just as I saw this, the cow started mooing like mad and backing up the hill. The dog went straight for her, and I was sure he was going to jump on her back like some wild animal or maybe grab the calf by the throat and kill it, but instead, he lowered himself and seemed to slide toward the cow and the calf, head down and ears flat. By this time, the cow had turned around and the calf was practically underneath it. The dog didn't bark or make any noise, and then he ran in and nipped the cow on the heel of one of its back hooves; then he started running to and fro below and behind the cow and calf, until the cow decided to move up the hill and the calf with her.

Daddy still hadn't seen this—he had the cows in the pasture and was getting off Lester to try and fix the fence. He shouted, "Abby! Abby!" I cantered Happy up the hill.

He said, "All you have to do is w—"

I said, "Look down the hill." Even from this high up, you could see the cow and the calf and the dog perfectly well.

I could tell that the last thing Daddy wanted to do was look down the hill—he sniffed, but then, there they were, cow mooing and calf bawling, both of them running up the hill with the dog at their heels. Daddy whooped and then laughed, standing there, holding Lester by the bridle.

The dog was good—he didn't just drive them straight. If he had, he would have run them into the fence. But he knew that they had to get where Daddy and Lester were, and so he went out to the right and got the cow to cross the hill. Daddy saw them coming and took Lester out of the way to the left of the gap, and that's where I stood, too. It took a few minutes, and my heart was beating, but it was like the dog never had any doubt about what was going to happen. He got the cow and the calf to where they were in front of the gap, and then the cow saw the other cows (and, of course, everyone was making an incredible racket), and then they ran through the gap and joined the others.

By this time, Mom had reached me where I was sitting on Happy, and she was laughing. "Did you see that?" she said, and the dog, who had stopped and was staring at the group of cows, looked over at her. That was what made me laugh. I was the one who was supposed to guard the gap on Happy while Daddy fixed the fence, but I didn't have to. That dog sat down maybe ten feet below the gap, right in the middle, just sat there with his tongue out of his mouth a bit but a confident look on his face, and believe me, those cows weren't going anywhere. When they moved more than he liked, he barked.

I got off Happy and gave the reins to Mom, and helped Daddy just a little bit. The posts weren't broken, but some of the wire was, so we strung four new strands and rolled up the old strands and Daddy stuck those in his saddlebag. When he mounted again and we walked down the hill, the dog didn't move for a long time—he just sat there, guarding the cows. It wasn't until we were almost to the gelding pen that I looked back up the hill and saw he was gone.

The horses were a little wild from all the activity and not having gotten their hay, but by the time we had fed them and put Lincoln, Happy, and Lester away, everything was calm and back to normal, except, of course, that it was nearly eleven o'clock and I was dead on my feet.

The next day, Mom let me sleep. And I did sleep—I looked at the clock when I woke up, and it read twenty after six. I thought I would look at the clock again, just to be sure, and it read half past ten, and the room was light, and I didn't have any sense of time having passed. When I sat up, I remembered Black George and the jumping and Jane Slater, and when I was in the bathroom, I remembered driving the cows up the hill in the moonlight, and then I remembered the dog. It wasn't until I was looking in my closet that I remembered that it was Monday and I had missed the school bus.

Mom came in from outside when I was getting the cereal down from the pantry, and she had a big smile on her face. She said, "Oh, you woke up! You must have been exhausted. I went in your room at seven, and you were so dead to the world, I just couldn't wake you."

I said, "What did Daddy say?"

"Not a word." She pointed to the ribbons and the trophy,

which one of them had set up on the sideboard. "He knows you did a good job. Yesterday *and* last night."

But she was still smiling. Then I happened to look out the kitchen door. There was a dog on the porch. There was *the* dog on the porch. I said, "Mom! Who is that?"

And she said, "Oh, you mean Rusty?"

"Rusty!"

She laughed.

The dog pricked his ears.

"How do you know his name is Rusty?"

"I think the real question is, how does *she* know her name is Rusty."

"How does she know?"

Mom shrugged. Then we went out on the porch.

Rusty was sitting over to the side, by one of the posts, looking out toward the barn. She did not rush to us when we opened the door but brushed her tail from side to side, and then, when Mom said, "Hey, Rusty," she stood up and walked over to us and sat down in front of us. Then she looked up at Mom and lifted her left paw. Mom took it.

I said, "She knows tricks?"

"She seems like a well-trained dog."

"She always looked so wild out there, like a wolf or something. I thought she was a he."

"Well, I'm thinking she's half German shepherd and maybe half Australian shepherd. She does have a wolfy look."

I said, "That's what I thought last night, when he—I mean she—started running after the cow and the calf. I thought she was going to attack them."

"Oh, I never once thought Rusty would do that."

Now I turned and stared at Mom. I said, "Have you known Rusty for a while, Mom?"

She gave me a big grin. "About four months now."

"That's since July."

"Yeah, that's about when she appeared."

"I thought we saw her the first time down at the crick a month or so ago."

"Well, she was following us."

"What does Daddy think?"

"After last night, your father said Rusty could live in the barn and be an outside dog."

"Your outside dog."

"Our outside dog."

"How long has Daddy known about her?"

"Oh, twelve hours, maybe."

Rusty was looking at me. She had a very steady gaze and dark golden eyes. Now she lifted her paw. I took it, and then petted her on the head and down her neck. I said, "She is awfully clean for a stray. And pretty fat, too."

"She's sleek, not fat. And I brush her, of course. I use one of the old body brushes. It gets through her coat nicely."

"But she is a little wolfy-looking."

"That's just the German shepherd in her." She petted her and stared at her with a happy look on her face, and I saw right then that Rusty was Mom's dog, and it didn't really matter what Daddy thought—Rusty had made up her mind. I said, "What are you feeding her?"

"Oh, vegetables. Leftovers if they aren't too rich. Rice

when we have it. She likes everything. I think she was scavenging before, and I think she was doing a pretty good job. Weren't you, Rusty?"

Rusty gave Mom her paw again.

The thing is, your mom is someone that you think you know. But Daddy always said about Mom, "Well, there's more there than meets the eye," and of course, he was right.

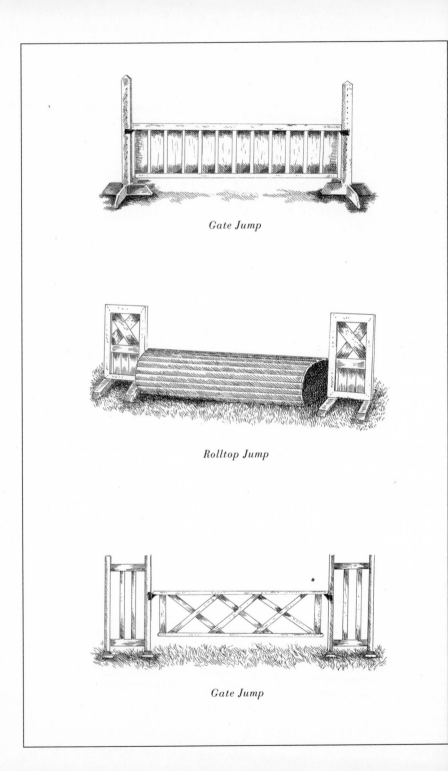

Gate Jump

Rolltop Jump

Gate Jump

Chapter 9

AFTER THE WEEKEND, THE WEEK AT SCHOOL WAS A REAL VACA-
tion. On Tuesday, Gloria, Stella, Leslie, Linda A., and Maria
and I all took the same school bus—number 6 rather than
number 9 for me—to Alexis and Barbara Goldman's house to
read *Julius Caesar* aloud. Barbara was going to "direct," and
Alexis was going to read the biggest part, which turned out to
be a character named Brutus. The villain, whose name was
Cassius, was assigned to Gloria. Alexis and Barbara said that
they didn't invite any boys because when Shakespeare was
writing, only boys and men were in the plays (boys played the
female parts), so it was only fair that our "production" (which
was what Barbara kept calling it) was all girls.

Alexis and Barbara lived just up the road from the school

bus stop, in a big house with lots of windows and a garden entirely made of large rocks, what looked like white gravel, and cactuses, instead of a front yard. As soon as we walked in, we saw that giant glass doors opened onto a deck that looked out over a valley to the back. If you went out onto the deck, you were standing on a cliff.

Alexis and Barbara shared two rooms right above this living room—they slept in bunk beds in one of the rooms and had the other for projects. This whole room was filled with shelves and cubbies, and they had two work areas—one was a table with art supplies on it, and the other was for music. Alexis's piano was there, and a music stand and a chair. Next to the chair was a table where Barbara kept her violin and her flute. I guess they thought that one violin plus one flute was equal to one piano.

There were chairs set up in the living room. A tray of cupcakes and a pitcher of lemonade sat on the coffee table. Mrs. Goldman said, "Oh, girls! Just relax and have a cupcake, and let Barbie take over, because she will, anyway!" And then Alexis, Barbara, and their mother laughed. There were also three cats—the two black ones in the house got up and scurried out as soon as they saw us, but the one on the deck stared in through the glass doors. It was an orange cat the size of a pillow. The others were much smaller.

We did let Barbara take over—it was easy. There were a lot more parts in the play than there were of us, so at the beginning of each scene, Barbara would assign each of us a role. Only Alexis and Gloria stayed the same. In the first scene, I played the Second Commoner, and I had to make a joke about shoes that I didn't understand until Barbara explained it to me. The second scene was where Julius came in—Linda A. played him. Maria played his wife, Calpurnia. I got to be the Soothsayer, who is the person who tells fortunes, and to say, "Beware the Ides of March!" Barbara had me say it in a deep, growly voice, and then Linda A. had to act afraid and repeat my sentence. It was at this point that we started to have fun.

Julius Caesar was not at all like *Great Expectations*. Even when I read the lines ahead of time and couldn't really figure them out, once we said them aloud, we did mostly understand them, and anyway, what was going to happen was pretty clear—Julius was going to get killed, and Cassius and Brutus were going to do the killing. Cassius wanted to and Brutus didn't really want to. There was one scene where Maria played someone named Casca and Linda A. played someone named Cicero. Cicero says hello to Casca, but Casca is very upset. For one thing, there has been an earthquake, and for another, Casca has seen some very scary things—a guy with fire coming out of his hand but his hand is not burning, a lion in the middle of town, and an owl screaming during daylight. Maria made it sound like a Frankenstein movie, and we were all staring at her—Linda A. was staring at her, too, just like she was scared to death. It was really fun.

Barbara and Alexis had been through the play already maybe three times, and they understood it perfectly as far as I could tell, so whenever one of us seemed confused, Barbara would stop things and very patiently explain what was going on. This meant that we did not get through the play on that first day. We only got to the scene where they actually kill

Julius, and we did that scene twice, once sitting in our chairs and once pushing the chairs back and acting it out. When we did it this way, Gloria got to fall down and say "Et tu, Brute!" which means, "You, too, Brutus!" Julius was surprised and upset because he thought Brutus was his friend. After that, Brutus and Cassius talk, and then I got to be a character called Antony, who is on the stage at the end with his servant, and he is the only one who is sorry to see Julius get stabbed. Since I was Antony, I had to pretend to go out early in the scene because one of Brutus and Cassius's friends lured me away so that they could get Julius.

It was dark by the time we were finished, and all of the cupcakes were gone. Mr. Goldman came home, and he and Mrs. Goldman watched us do the last scene, then clapped and shouted, "Bravo! Bravo!" so we were all laughing and excited by the time the parents showed up. Gloria's mom came in and watched and clapped, too, and then I went to their car, because Gloria's mom was giving me a ride. All the way to my house, she talked about how great the Goldmans were, and it was true. The plan was to go back Saturday and finish the play.

When I got home, it was after dark and Daddy had done all the work. He and Mom had ridden Lester and Sprinkles and Jefferson and Lincoln down to the crick. Lester seemed fine after his busy night Sunday, and Daddy had gotten Black George out and trotted him around a bit to see how he felt after the show. "Perfectly sound and not at all tired, as far as I can see." Daddy ate a bite of his pork chop. He said, "You sure you showed that horse, Abby?"

"More than that."

"What do you mean?"

"Jane—that's what Miss Slater wants me to call her now—had us jump some bigger jumps in the afternoon. I meant to tell you that, but I was too tired to remember."

"How big?" said Mom, setting down her fork.

"Well . . ." I could tell that Daddy wanted to know, but Mom really didn't. I said, "Maybe . . . maybe four feet." I scraped my fork around on my plate where the mashed potatoes had been.

Mom said, "That's like jumping out of the pasture out there."

"No, it isn't," said Daddy. "Those are four-six."

"I don't know—" said Mom, but Daddy said, "How did it feel?"

"Black George doesn't care." I looked at the two of them, Mom a little white and Daddy a little excited. I wished Mom would start eating again. After a moment, I said, "While we were doing it, I didn't really realize how high they were. He just gallops down and jumps them." I thought about the two ways I had felt about those jumps—that they were easy and that they were scary. How could they be both at the same time? So I said, "They were easy."

"Oh dear," said Mom. But she started eating again. She took a bite of salad.

It was funny the way her saying that made me both more confident and more scared at exactly the same time. But I thought if she knew I was scared, she would get more scared and make me stop jumping so high. I didn't want to stop. I said, "You just get in the rhythm. Jane—Miss Slater—said she can't believe what good horses we have."

"We've had some luck this year, I think," said Daddy. "Not every year is a lucky one, but the Lord does provide." When he said this, Mom glanced out the back door. Rusty now had a blanket all her own on the porch and another blanket all her own, an old woolen horse blanket, in the barn. I could see her on her new blanket, her paws neatly together and her chin resting on them, but her ears up and her eyes bright, keeping an eye on things. I realized that that was what she had been doing since I first saw her, keeping an eye on things. Mom saw me looking at her and smiled.

Daddy said, "Which brings me to Lester."

"Lester is such a good horse," said Mom.

"I have a buyer for Lester."

"That's too bad," said Mom.

Daddy shrugged, then said, "Jack Louis came down this morning to talk about the fence, and I was grooming Lester. He asked if he's for sale, and I had to say yes, so he tried him. He liked him a little too much in the opinion of my heart, but just enough in the opinion of our bank account."

I said, "How much did he like him?"

"He offered two thousand."

"Gracious!" said Mom.

"Well, he's a good horse. Chased those cows up the hill and thought nothing of it," said Daddy. "We don't get to keep the really good ones, no matter how much we like them." He caught my eye.

I said, "I know that, Daddy."

He said, "We all know that."

Well, we did know that, but it was a lesson I kept having to learn. After supper, I went out to the gelding pasture. I tried to be quiet, but Jack saw me, anyway, and nickered. Even so, he didn't come over. He and Black George were finishing all the bits of hay they could find from every pile—it was like they were vacuuming. Lester and Jefferson were standing together, switching flies, and Lincoln was having a drink. All of a sudden, Jack reached toward Black George and gave him a little nip, then he jumped backward when Black George snorted and pinned his ears. Then he waited a moment, but when Black George went back to nosing the ground for hay, he stepped forward again and gave him a little nip on the haunches. Black George now pinned his ears and lifted his back end, as if to kick, but he didn't raise his feet. He was saying, "I could kick you. Don't make me."

But Jack seemed determined to make him, because he trotted around to the other side and nipped him again, then he spun and cantered off. This time, Black George seemed to think that Jack was determined to be a pest, so he chased after him a few feet with his ears pinned, and then it looked like he decided to get in the game, because he picked up speed and caught up to Jack and reached out to nip him. Jack immediately turned and reared up, and so Black George reared up, and they tossed their heads at one another and squealed. They lifted their forelegs, but not as if they really meant it, and then Black George came down and galloped off, and Jack ran after him. Once he caught up (and he did that very quickly), the two of them took off around the fence line of the pasture, bucking and kicking.

It made me laugh to see them play, and reminded me that

the way I had been thinking of Black George at the show, as my perfect machine of a horse who just goes and goes and does whatever you ask so that you can sort of ignore him, was wrong. I knew right then all over again that Black George had his own ideas of what was fun and how to do his job. I thought that with just one bit of effort, I could see the courses we were jumping from his point of view, and that point of view would be lower than mine, but wider—he would see everything all around us, but nothing right in front of us or right behind us. And he would feel the earth under his feet, and he would hear lots more sounds than I could hear, as he flicked his ears back and forth. And he would feel me on his back.

The best thing about Black George—I thought I should always remember this—was that all those sensations that he had were fun for him. So he was not a machine, but a horse who enjoyed himself most of the time, even when, as now, Jack was racing toward him with his head down and his tail down, as if he were going to run right into him. But he didn't. The two of them just reared up again and galloped past Lester and Jefferson, who pinned their ears and insisted on being left alone. So I called Jack over to the fence, and Black George came with him, and I gave them each a piece of apple. Then the others looked at us and decided that they had to know what was going on, so in about two seconds, I was surrounded by horses and handing out everything in my pockets, which wasn't much.

It was Thursday when the next letter arrived from Mr. Brandt. It was a long one, and when I brought it in from the mailbox,

I really wanted to open it. It made me nervous. But I was too nervous to open it, so I didn't carry it out to Daddy. I set it on the table and went to my room to put on my riding clothes.

We worked three horses each. It looked like this was going to be Daddy's last ride on Lester, so we took him and Happy up the hill to see the cows. The fence was really fixed now—five strands of wire and some extra posts all along the section where they got out, because they never forget where it was that they did that once they've made it. Daddy said, "Some cows can jump, you know, just like a horse, but maybe these haven't figured that out."

I said, "Happy could really take to that cow-chasing thing."

"That's my next project, roping off of her."

"I wondered why you got out the sawcow." The sawcow was like a sawhorse, but it had sides painted like a cow, and it had horns.

Daddy said, "We'll start slow. Something fun to do for a few weeks."

Then we took Sprinkles and Black George down to the crick, and finally, we rode Jefferson and Lincoln in the arena. The problem with them was getting them going, not controlling them, so at least once or twice a week, we had to make sure that they walked, trotted, and cantered nicely. Jem Jarrow's way of getting a horse to step under and loosen up was good for that, too, even though Jefferson and Lincoln were never grumpy, just lazy.

When we put them away, I rubbed Jack down while he was eating his evening hay and Daddy was dragging the hose around to fill the water tanks, and all in all, I just forgot about the letter until I walked in the house and saw that Mom had opened it already, and it was lying there waiting for me. I picked it up. It read:

Dear Mr. Lovitt,

We have made considerable progress in our investigation into the disappearance of Alabama Lady, and I thought that I would bring you up to date on what we have found, as there is a possibility that something we have learned might trigger your memory in some way. We still have not heard from the party who purchased the other mare at By Golly Horse Sales, and now there appears to be a third mare of a similar description who was found somewhat closer to Wheatsheaf Ranch, but we have had little luck in tracing that mare as well.

The story as we now understand it:

Here in Texas, where the Wheatsheaf Ranch is located, October 14 of last year was an unusually hot day—Indian summer, which around here means in the nineties and humid. For this reason, Allan Wilkes, the farm manager, decided to leave the mares out in the larger fields, where they could stay cooler, rather than doing what he normally does in cooler weather, which is to gather them in smaller pens closer to the barns for the night.

The mares, therefore, were given a good feed of hay, and all the gates were checked and found to be locked with padlocks at approximately five p.m. Alabama Lady and four other mares occupied a particular pasture close to the road and some distance from the hay barn. There are three other pastures close by. Each of these pastures contained between three and six pregnant mares.

At approximately midnight, Isabella Marquez, the wife of one of the foaling grooms, whose apartment is somewhat close to the road, remembers waking up to the sound of a truck engine slowing on the road, then stopping, then starting up again. Although this is not an uncommon occurrence near the ranch, given subsequent events, this evidence is considered to be significant in this investigation.

Sunrise the following morning, October 15, took place approximately six-thirty a.m. central standard time, at which point two workers, Mario Marquez and Sergio Marquez, Mario's son, noticed that one of the pastures was empty. They subsequently found that the fence had been dismantled at the corner closest to the road—the nails holding the boards to the posts had been pried loose and the boards tossed in a ditch nearby. All five mares had disappeared. It was first assumed that all five mares had been stolen and taken away in some sort of trailer or van. Unfortunately, the weather had been dry, and there was no readable evidence in the dirt of the road of who the thieves might be or what their subsequent movements were.

Of the five mares in the pasture, four were rather young. The fifth was sixteen years old and in foal to one of the stallions standing at the ranch. Although she was a particular favorite of Mr. Matthews, she was the least valuable of the five mares, and, fortunately, she was the first to be found. It is possible that she was left behind by the thieves, because she was discovered not far down the road, nuzzling some other mares across the fence at the far end of the ranch. She was in good shape and not injured in any way.

In addition to Alabama Lady, the other three mares were a chestnut with a white blaze and one white foot, named Lucy Lightfoot, in foal to a Kentucky stallion named Dedicate; a gray mare named Morethanenough, in foal to Sword Dancer; and another chestnut mare with a star and an idiosyncratic snip that ran up between her nostrils, then around the side of her face, named Leonia, also in foal to Dedicate. The fourth, of course, was Alabama Lady, the largest of the five mares, in foal, as I have said, to Jaipur. That the thieves should have focused on these four mares could indicate that they knew their way around Mr. Matthews's operation. We have pursued a number of leads in this regard, and of course, every large business must have disgruntled former employees to watch out for.

Mario Marquez reported the theft before seven a.m., and police arrived at the scene by eight. Mr. Matthews was informed of the theft by telephone in London, England, where he had traveled on business a week earlier. When the police could make no headway in finding the four younger mares in the subsequent forty-eight hours, my firm was enlisted to help in the investigation.

Because the older mare was found, the local police

assumed that the theft was actually an act of vandalism and spent most of the next two days looking around the area for the four mares. As you may know, the area is ranch country, with few roads and lots of rangeland for cattle. It was thought likely that the mares would have taken refuge somewhere nearby, where there was hay and water. Local ranchers were enlisted to help with the search, and one man offered his small crop-dusting plane, but the mares were not found. At this point, I think it was likely that they were hidden somewhere. Perhaps you never realize how huge a landscape is until you are looking for several horses under a tree or down in a draw.

As soon as my firm entered the investigation, we decided to treat the disappearance as a theft. The difficult question is, what could a thief do with four expensive Thoroughbred mares in foal to four expensive stallions? and the answer to that question is, not much. All Thoroughbreds have pedigrees, and all Thoroughbred pedigrees are unique. All breeding stallions and mares are registered, and a stallion and a mare can only come together one time in a single year, and so any attempt to sell these mares and these foals as themselves would result in their being identified as stolen animals. Nor could they be raced anywhere in the world, since the system of Thoroughbred racing is worldwide, and registration papers with the various jockey clubs of the various racing countries are required in order for a horse to go to the racetrack and be entered in races.

The only hope that a thief would have of putting

these mares' offspring to use would be to use them as ringers—that is, to substitute these well-bred foals for other foals similarly marked but of lesser breeding, and to put them in races at long odds in order to make money on large bets, but although this is a possible plot, it seems like an expensive and elaborate one not guaranteed to result in rapid or certain reward. I confess that given the nature of Thoroughbred horse racing, I was perplexed as to the motive of the thieves, if, indeed, they were thieves rather than vandals.

My firm did, of course, contact every horse auction facility and sale barn in Texas, and we also perused periodicals devoted to horse trading. On the thirtieth of October, we were alerted to the presence of a mare in an auction in West Texas, and a representative of our firm did go to that town and identify the pregnant mare as Mr. Matthews's mare Leonia by the snip that curls around her nose.

She was not in as good a condition as we would have wished, and the manager of the horse auction said that he had received her from a man of average height and build, with a northern accent of some sort, who said that he had run out of money and could no longer feed his horse, and so he had to sell her for what he could get. The auction manager gave him two hundred dollars, thinking that he got a good deal for a nice mare who just needed some weight. The unknown man left in his truck, with his trailer. The auction manager did not think to get his license plate number. The man did sign a paper, but he scribbled the name "Sonny Liston," obviously not his own.

Leonia was quickly returned to Wheatsheaf Ranch and is in good health. She produced a filly in March of this year. After her reappearance, Mr. Matthews decided to offer a reward for the return of the other mares, five hundred dollars apiece. For one week, we heard nothing of note.

It was the fact that we found the mare Lucy Lightfoot at a farm in Arkansas that alerted us that the thieves, whoever they were, had abandoned the mares. The mare seemed to have been left by the side of Route 375 and to have wandered about before showing up at the farm of Walter Brinkhorn, near the small town of Mena. She was discovered one morning foraging in a harvested cornfield. She was in somewhat worse condition than Leonia, with an injury to her eye and another injury to her left ankle that looked like it had been caused by barbed wire. After we were satisfied that Walter Brinkhorn had indeed found the mare, we paid him his reward. Unfortunately, the mare suffered a tetanus infection from neglect of the wound to her ankle and could not be saved. She died at the ranch shortly after returning home. The foal, of course, could not be saved, either, as it was only at a gestational age of six months.

Two days later, the third mare, the gray mare Morethanenough, also turned up, but her fate was happier than that of Lucy Lightfoot. She was found near

Fort Worth, on a horse farm, in a pasture with twelve other mares. The owners had been out of town for two weeks, leaving the care of the farm to a manager and two grooms. The groom in charge of the mare pasture did not notice the addition of a thirteenth mare, especially as four of the mares were gray and one of them looked rather like Morethanenough. When they did notice her, it took several days for them to connect her with the reward notices for Mr. Matthews's lost mare, but they turned her over readily, and there is no reason to doubt either the story of the farm owners (respected members of Dallas–Fort Worth society) or the grooms. Morethanenough was not as far along in her pregnancy as the others, and she produced a healthy colt last May.

The remaining mare, Alabama Lady, has simply disappeared from view. My guess is that the thieves, realizing that they could not profit from their theft, drove around Texas and abandoned the mares in widely separated regions, and that the mares then foraged on their own for days or weeks. Leonia was found hundreds of miles from Lucy Lightfoot and hundreds of miles from Morethanenough. If, indeed, Alabama Lady is the mare that you purchased from By Golly Horse Sales, then that location is, once again, hundreds of miles from both Wheatsheaf Ranch and the locations where the other mares were found.

Records at By Golly Horse Sales indicate that a brown mare was purchased on November 6 from a man who found her in Cheyenne and Arapaho country. She was in bad shape, so he sold her to By Golly Horse Sales for $125. The young man who received the horse and paid for her did not remember to ask for a receipt for the cash he paid, so there is no record of who sold her to By Golly. She was turned out with the other mares, and the young man does not remember anything specific about her, except that "she seemed real hungry and thirsty." Once she was turned out with the other twenty mares at the horse sales, no one noticed her in particular. She was one of four brown mares with no white markings. These were dispersed by the end of November.

I have since driven around the Cheyenne and Arapaho country. As you may know, that area is arid and in many ways desolate, with few towns. I did not expect to find the man who sold the horse to By Golly Horse Sales, and I did not find him. My work on another investigation may bring me to California in the near future. If so, I would like to visit you at your ranch and discuss your memories of Alabama Lady at the time when you saw her at By Golly Horse Sales and bought her. I would also like to have a look at her colt. I hope that this is acceptable to you. Please let me know.

Yours truly,
Howard W. Brandt

While I was reading this letter, Mom was finishing cooking dinner—macaroni and cheese. She didn't make me set the table; she just let me read the letter. When I was through, I put the pages together and laid them on the sideboard. I thought it was sad, thinking of those mares being driven all around the countryside, and maybe not fed, and then just being let go, one by one, far away from each other so they didn't even have friends. I had read a book once in which a girl wants a horse, so she tames a white mare who happens to be running around the neighborhood of her family farm. I must have been ten when I read that book. When I was ten, I thought the part that was hard to believe was that if she wanted a horse and she lived on a farm, why didn't she just go to a horse auction and buy one? But now that I was thirteen, I knew that not everyone can have a horse, even if they live on a farm. Now I thought the part that was hard to believe was that the horse would be by herself, that she would not want to make friends and be taken into the barn and given some hay and a brushing.

Thinking about that book made me think about Brown Jewel, and thinking about Brown Jewel made me think about that book—that lonely horse running around, not really knowing what to do.

When we sat down at the table, I asked Daddy what the Cheyenne and Arapaho country was like. He said, "Well, it's plains. Arid and dry. Good farming country in places, though. Good wheat country."

"But if Brown Jewel was lost there—"

"Well, maybe she wasn't lost for very long."

"If they stole her on October fifteenth, and the first mare was found before October thirtieth, then they could have been abandoned for two or three weeks."

"They could have," said Daddy. "But by the time I saw her, she didn't look as thin as that. I don't know that she got the kind of feed we would give her, but she must have gotten something."

"Yes," said Mom. "I don't think you should think of her as wandering around lost. Besides, we don't know that the mare we had was the mare that was lost. Mr. Brandt says that a couple of times. Our mare could have been just a mare that a rancher had and needed to get rid of, like all the others we find. Like Black George and Happy. The world is full of people who realize all of a sudden that they have too many horses."

I almost said, But what about the cowlick? I didn't say that. It seemed like Mom and Daddy were interested in the mare, but that they really, really were not sure that Pearl was this Alabama Lady, while I was really, really sure that Pearl was Alabama Lady and Jack was the son of Jaipur. I didn't want to be sure of that, but I was.

But I also didn't want to persuade them that what I thought was true, and after this, I shut up, and we talked about taking Black George out to the stable for a training session in a week, when we had a day off school for teacher training.

I knew about Oklahoma—or I knew about the part of Oklahoma where my grandparents lived, which was more to the east, and pretty green, with lots of cricks and rivers, and much more rain than we had in California, at least in good times. Even though my father and his brothers grew up ranching, riding, and roping cattle, not everyone they knew had ranches—some had farms and grew crops, and what you did depended a little on what sort of land you had and a little on what you liked to grow. My grandparents Lovitt sometimes talked about the Dust Bowl, when it seemed like all their neighbors left Oklahoma for somewhere else, and they would say, "Well, it was bad, but we survived it, and thank the Lord for that." My uncle Luke liked to tease Daddy by saying that the only reason he moved to California was that he had missed the train the first time around because he was only a baby when it left before, and he was too little to climb the step. Mom's family was from farther east, really green country with woods, almost to the Ozark Mountains, and the way Daddy teased her was to say that her grandfather never did realize that he'd got out of Missouri all the way to Oklahoma—he died thinking he was still twenty miles from Springfield. All of these things were completely familiar to me.

After supper, I did my usual things—I studied *le subjonctif*— "*J'aimerais que vous m'appeliez demain*," which was, "I would like for you to do something or other tomorrow." I read about the Ohio River Valley and Tippecanoe and Tyler, too. I looked at pictures of the circulatory system. And I solved eighteen math problems, such as "John is two years older than three times Joe's age. If Joe is *x* years old, how would you calculate John's age?" I didn't have to read *Julius Caesar* because we were going to finish that Saturday at the Goldmans' house, and actually, I was looking forward to that.

It was a cool night, so I put on my jacket and went out to say goodnight to Jack, Black George, Happy, and Sprinkles. Lester was gone—he had left that day. The gelding pasture looked a little empty without his bright buckskin beauty. By the time I got to bed, I thought I had forgotten completely about that letter—I didn't feel bad and I went right to sleep, but in the middle of the night, I dreamt about Pearl.

She was on the hillside above the ranch, not far from where the cows had broken through the fence. Even though I knew that she was there, I also saw that the hillside was much bigger than usual—it was a real mountain, like in the sierras or something. Pearl was crossing it, not going up or down, but making her way along it, stopping from time to time to taste the grass. The grass was brown and thin, almost just dirt. She was above the gelding pasture, in a way, but instead of our geldings in it, there was just the stubble of some harvested crop. In the dream, I knew it was "peat," but I had no idea what "peat" was—something not very edible, since Pearl didn't even try to get to it. She stopped under a tree, but the tree got smaller, so she walked on. I knew in the dream that there wasn't any water anywhere, and that she was thirsty—she hadn't had water in three weeks. A voice that sounded like mine in the dream said that that was impossible, that she couldn't be walking if she hadn't had water in three weeks, and then Mom's voice said, "Well, you'd be surprised."

She walked, and then she stumbled and went to her knees, and then she got up and walked again, but she wasn't getting anywhere—the hill just seemed to go on and on. In the dream, I thought she should come down the hill and get some water at our place, but there was no way to tell Pearl this. As I watched her in the dream, I didn't see anything else—no cows, no other horses, no people, and no dogs or coyotes—no one. And then she fell again, but this time she rolled down the hill, she rolled and rolled over and over (though I don't know how a horse could do that—it was as if she were a stuffed animal), and I was shocked and upset. At the bottom of the hill, she stopped rolling, and she lay there, and as she lay there, she looked exactly the way she had when we found her the day she died, stretched out on the ground, the hair rubbed off her forehead, her tongue hanging out of her mouth just a little bit, and her eyes half closed. Jack wasn't born, or wasn't around, or something. She was completely alone.

I woke up from this dream crying. I was heaving deep breaths, and the tears were pouring out of my eyes, and I could hear myself and feel how wet my face was, and it took me a few minutes (I don't know how many) to realize that it was a dream. I wiped my face with the corner of my sheet.

My clock read four a.m. I was still taking deep breaths. Pearl lying there was so in my head that I felt like I had to get up and look out the window, try and look across the gelding pasture and just see for myself whether she was really not there. But actually getting up and checking seemed bad, like giving in to temptation, so I lay there with my arms outside the covers, holding myself in the bed, and I told myself that my dream of Pearl had nothing to do with what had happened to her, really. There was no way of knowing what had happened to her, or rather, what had happened to her was that Daddy bought her, and she came to us, and for almost two months, she had plenty to eat and other horses to be with and us, Daddy, Mom, and me, who treated her kindly and were just waiting for things with the other horses to slow down before riding her. But then I remembered that what really happened to her was that she gave birth and a month later colicked and died, and we had been unable to save her or even to help her, and then I felt like no time had really passed since that day, and then I was crying again.

So now I did get up, and I went to the window and looked out. There was no moon, and I couldn't see the horses except as dark shapes not very distinguishable from other dark shapes, so I opened the window, and in rolled the fragrance of the ranch—of the wind off the hillside, of the paddocks and the horses, of some additional freshness that I couldn't identify. It was cool—or cold—and it woke me up. I felt Pearl go out of my head, and I knew that rolling down the hill hadn't happened. A horse whinnied, and then another one whinnied back, then another one snorted and another one groaned the way horses do when they are getting up from lying down. Sure enough, I could just make out one of the horses in the gelding pasture pulling himself to his feet and then shaking himself off and blowing air out of his nostrils. He must have been asleep. Just looking at the geldings in the pasture, all of them doing this and that, no big deal, made me feel calmer. It was now almost four-thirty. I yawned and went back to bed.

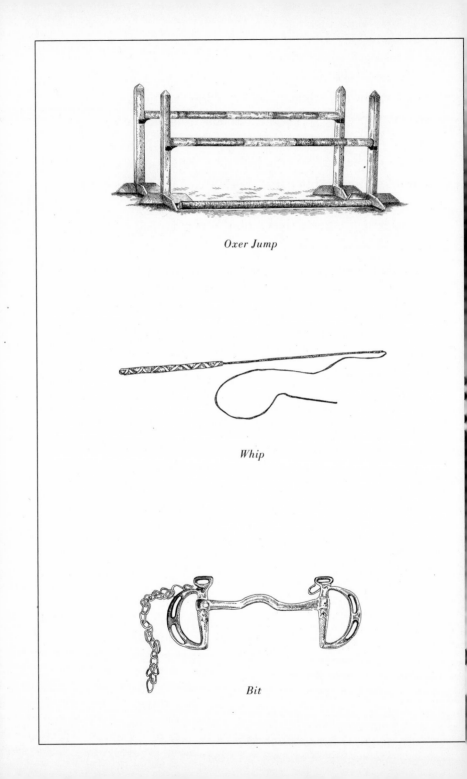

Oxer Jump

Whip

Bit

Chapter 10

But it's funny how a feeling sticks in your mind. Everything is the same, but it looks a little different just because of
that feeling. For me, for the next couple of days, things just
looked a little sadder than usual. Here was Rusty, who got to lie
on the porch now and be petted by Mom, and called by her
new name, which she seemed to understand, and instead of
thinking of her as a dog who had found a home, I thought of
her as a dog who had looked for a home for a long time. Or
here was Stella in a new outfit (a green and black plaid skirt
with a round-collared pink blouse, which actually looked
pretty nice with the plaid), and I didn't think of her as a girl
with a new outfit but as a girl who was never satisfied, no matter how many outfits her mom bought her. Here was Kyle

Gonzalez, who always got As, which was how I usually thought of him, but now it seemed to me that As would never be good enough for him. Or there was Leslie. Leslie always sat near people but never right with them. She could have opened her mouth and said something, or she could have sat in a corner and read a book, but she did the one thing that was guaranteed to make her feel left out.

Only Alexis and Barbara could not be made to be unhappy. You could see it in the way they walked down the hall—they were always talking to one another about their plans. Yakety-yak, yakety-yak—they would stride down the hall and just slide around whoever was in their way without even noticing. "Excuse me; oh, sorry; hi; thanks"—there was a way that they were perfectly polite, because they knew all the words and said them automatically, but they didn't look around themselves. I realized that they were so full of projects that maybe it never crossed their minds to wonder what the other kids thought of them, or who liked them and who didn't. They had each other.

On Friday, efficient as always, they came up to each of us who was going to be at the play-reading on Saturday and handed us index cards with our name, the time, and the parts we would read. It was not like they were telling us what to do—it was like they were letting us in on their plans, their fun. They smiled and laughed and said, "Oh, Abby, this is going to be such a good time! Mom gave us a bunch of old sheets and some cord, and she said we could make them into togas if we don't tear them or anything, so we set the time for fifteen minutes early, so we can put them on!"

I was Antony, mostly, with a few centurions and other

people who just had to say a word or two. That night, I did a lot of horse work that I would normally have done on Saturday morning, but really, Daddy didn't care, because he had heard of both Shakespeare and *Julius Caesar* and he never minded me getting an A in school. Mom dropped me at the Goldmans' at nine-fifteen Saturday morning and said she would be back at noon.

The big living room was set up more like a theater. They had laid down some sheets of wood up against the window, so that the valley outside looked like the backdrop, and they had set up about ten or twelve chairs in front of the stage for an audience. Gloria and I must have looked a little nervous about this, because Mrs. Goldman walked past us, carrying a bowl of cut-up fruit, and said, "Oh, girls! Won't this be fun? Even a little bitty audience just raises your energy, somehow. And the neighbors kept asking if they could come over and have a look." She set the fruit down next to some drop doughnuts and biscuits.

After we had had what we wanted of the treats, we went into the dining room, where Mrs. Goldman and one of the neighbors pinned our togas on us. They felt silly, but I have to say that when we all came out into the living room and stood in the stage, we looked pretty good. Alexis's toga was yellow, because they had run out of white sheets, but she had also found a plastic sword, which she had in a loop at her waist.

We started where we had left off Tuesday—Julius was dead, and everyone had to talk about him and say why they had killed him. First up was Alexis, as Brutus, who made a speech about how much he loved Julius, but how much he thought Julius was about to take over the country and become a dictator, and he felt he had to stop that. All the girls in their togas said they thought this was about right, and it was a good thing that Julius had been killed.

Then it was my turn. I was nervous because I had so many speeches to read, but I knew if I got mixed up, Barbara would stop us and tell me what was going on. The first thing I had to say was "Friends, Romans, Countrymen, lend me your ears, I come to bury Caesar, not to praise him." Then I went on about how Brutus and Cassius and the other ones who killed Julius had good reasons, and were good men, and then I went back to all the good things that Julius had done, and what a nice person he was, and then I said that I wasn't going to say too many good things about Julius, just a few. This went on and on. It was a long scene, and at one point, I stepped on my toga, and it started to fall off, so I had to hold it to myself with my arm and pretend that I just couldn't go on any longer. By the end, though, after I read Julius's will, in which he gave every Roman some money and also a park, I had the Romans completely worked up and ready to go kill Brutus and Cassius and their friends.

After that, there was a scene where the Romans mean to kill one of the assassins, but they kill another guy with the same name instead, and then there is a war. I had a lot of scenes in the war. My friend Octavius, who is Julius's son, and I win the war, and the last thing that happens is that Alexis as Brutus falls on her sword and kills herself, and then I say what a great person Brutus was, that his intentions were always good and noble, even though those of, say, Cassius, or even me, myself, as Antony, were not.

It took us until after noon to finish this, and by that time, Mom had come in and was sitting in a chair. When we were finished, everyone clapped and shouted "Bravo!" and "Hurray," and we took three bows, with Alexis and Barbara taking four.

When I was in the dining room taking off my toga, Barbara came up to me, and took my hands between hers, and said, "Oh, Abby! You were so good! I really liked watching you." And she gave me a hug and a kiss on the cheek. I didn't know what to say, so I just said, "Well, I understand this play better than I ever understood any book we've read for English before, and that's because of you." And it was true—when we took our test on *Julius Caesar* that week, I thought it was easy, and I got a hundred on it.

But Mom didn't like it as much as I did. Once we had gotten into the car and were maybe five minutes down the road, she said, "My, that was surprising, the way Barbara, was it? had to kill herself at the end there."

"That was Alexis. Barbara was our director."

"Alexis, then. I'm not sure that was really a suitable story for you kids."

"Well, it was Shakespeare."

"I know that."

"It was assigned. The whole eighth grade has to read it. In *Great Expectations*, the little boy gets beaten all the time by his sister, and then at the end, the bad guy is killed and the other guy dies just before they are going to hang him." I looked at Mom, whose eyebrows were a little lifted. Then I said, "Of course, I didn't understand what was going on while I was reading it. So it didn't make much of an impact."

Mom chuckled, but then she got serious again. She said, "You girls actually acted out these crimes, though. That's a little different."

We did act them out, I thought, and it was fun. And it wasn't really fun until we got to those parts of the play. But I didn't say this. I didn't know what to say until I said, "Well, my character didn't take part in the murders."

"I'm glad of that."

"But there was a scene before you got there where because of things he said, the citizens killed an innocent person."

"I think I need to talk to your teacher."

I said, "An innocent person like Jesus."

Mom looked at me.

I said, "Didn't you read Shakespeare at school?"

"We read *A Midsummer Night's Dream* in tenth grade, *Hamlet* in eleventh grade, and *Macbeth* in twelfth grade."

"Did you believe them?"

"Well, we *read* them, we didn't act them out. And I don't know that I actually read them all the way through." She looked at me. "Though I can't believe I'm admitting that." We laughed a little, then we were quiet for a while, until I said, "Barbara thought I was good."

"You were good. I thought so, too. That's probably why I'm worried all of a sudden. And Alexis was good. I believed that she was killing herself." She looked at me. "Sort of."

"Everybody got really into it, even Leslie. And Maria. Maria had the spookiest lines, and it sort of gave you the willies to listen to her. What I liked about my part was, I don't know, that I had to think of what happened in two ways at the same time—that there was a good side to the fact that they killed Julius and a bad side to it, and that there was a good side to me, because I loved Julius, but a bad side to me, too, because I wanted to get even with them for killing Julius, but then at the end, I realized that even though Brutus had killed Julius and I was really mad at him for that, he really did think he was doing the right thing."

Mom didn't say anything to this—we were almost home. But it was true. When things really started to happen, how were you going to make up your mind what to do? If you have a good side and a bad side, then how do you choose if there are lions walking around downtown and people are lit on fire without burning up, the way they were in *Julius Caesar*? I sighed. We turned into our driveway. Mom said, "Well, honey, I can see you are growing up." When she stopped the car at the gate, she said, "I don't know that that's a good thing. But there's nothing we can do about it, is there?" She leaned over and gave me a kiss before I got out to open the gate. When Daddy asked me how the play went, I noticed that she didn't say anything. I said it was fun.

On Monday, it started raining and rained for three days, the first rains of the year, and a little early. Daddy and Mom were happy about this, and so, I suppose, were the horses, but for me, it was bad because when I brought out my sweaters and my raincoat, they were all too small. And Mom didn't have time to take me to the store until the weekend, and so the choice was wearing one of Danny's old sweaters or trying to fit into mine, which was uncomfortable across the shoulders and the chest. I did have to wear Danny's old raincoat, which was incredibly wide and an ugly green color like pea soup. Gloria and

Stella had both thought ahead and had new raincoats. Gloria's was tan, with a belt, and Stella's was yellow, with black polka dots. It had a black corduroy collar and a matching rain hat and was very cute. They were so proud of them that during lunch, they ate fast and then paraded around outside just to show them off. Me, I went into our homeroom and did some homework.

Thursday and Friday were teacher training days, so on Thursday morning, Daddy and I loaded up Black George and headed out to Jane Slater for another lesson. I was really happy that it wasn't raining, even though, at the coast, it was gloomy and cold. Miss Slater was glad to see us, and as soon as we unloaded Black George and were tacking him up, she brought Colonel Hawkins over. Colonel Hawkins walked right up to Daddy and shook his hand, and said, "Great to have you here, Mr. Lovitt. Jane tells me you have some nice horses."

"We think so," said Daddy. "Most of them are ranch horses, though."

Colonel Hawkins was standing, staring at Black George, one hand on his hip and the other one stroking his chin. He had on black breeches and the most beautiful boots I had ever seen, deep reddish brown with three buckles down the sides and tied like shoes across the ankle. They were perfectly polished but so old and used that they just folded around his legs. He said, "This fellow is not a ranch horse."

"No," said Daddy, "I figured that one out. But no telling what his breeding is. I got him the same place as all the others, out in Oklahoma."

"Well," said Colonel Hawkins, "when I was at Fort Riley, in the U.S. Cavalry, we got good horses from Oklahoma all the time. There are good horses everywhere, if you've got time to go look for them."

"Fort Riley is in Kansas," said Daddy, "so I suppose that's true."

Kansas and Oklahoma were right next to each other, of course. Daddy and Colonel Hawkins smiled at each other.

Now the colonel walked slowly around Black George, first clockwise, then counter-clockwise, looking at him very carefully, but he didn't touch him. Black George stood up nicely, his ears either flopped in a relaxed way or pricked, if something seemed to be happening over by the barn. Finally, Colonel Hawkins said, "Thank you," and stepped up to Black George, patted him on the nose, and palmed him a lump of sugar, saying, "Good boy." Then he said, "Jane, we'll talk later," and "Abby, Mr. Lovitt, a pleasure to meet you."

"Oh," said Jane once he left. "Such a clammy day. I've been cold since I woke up. I think we need to get moving."

She led us over to the big ring, the main one where they had the horse show, and Daddy gave me a leg up into the saddle. Black George seemed to be saying, "Ah, I've been here before," as he ambled around, looking at this and that—more at the trees and what was happening in the distance than at the jumps. The jumps did not surprise him. I was enjoying myself, but I could see Daddy and Jane talking a mile a minute. At one point, as I was trotting by, I heard Daddy say "Wow," and I thought, "Uh-oh," though I didn't know why. Then Rodney Lemon showed up, leaning on the railing around the corner of the ring near the barns. As I trotted by, he called out, "Hey, lass! Nice horse you got there!"

I waved.

Jane came into the ring, and I went over to her. She said, "Now, Abby, I want this to be a very relaxed sort of day for him. Just make some big trot circles and weave around the jumps. Get him to balance up, but don't make a big deal of it."

We did this. The very best thing about riding a good horse who wants to do what you ask and can do what you ask is that it feels really good when he does it. It feels easy and buoyant and like both of you are happy, and if you weren't happy before it started feeling good, then pretty soon you are happy, because it is feeling good.

Jane went over to one of the jumps, set by itself along the far end of the ring, and made a crossbar, then put a pole out in front of it. I was to trot the pole to the crossbar. It was easy. Daddy came in the ring to help her, but then he just stood there—she was so quick at setting jumps that it was easier to do it herself than to tell him what to do. She bustled around, putting up a two-stride in-and-out, raising the original crossbar, dragging a gate and a couple of standards into place. Pretty soon she had a course made, of eight jumps, which used part of the course that was already in the ring and was partly new. In the meantime, I had warmed Black George up over about six small jumps, and I could tell he was ready for something more fun.

She gave me the course and helped me walk it with my fingers—it wasn't that complicated: two loops, then out to the two-stride, and around over the brush, finishing over the original crossbar, which was now a vertical. Everything looked small, and the first time around, that was the problem—Black George wasn't impressed by the size of the jumps, and so he didn't bother to set himself up or get organized.

Jane and Daddy were in the middle of the arena. She said, "Now, he's fine but careless. In that case, you need to shorten your reins a little, sit up, raising your hands up a little, and go straight to the middle of every fence, just to show him that even though he's not impressed, there's still a discipline to every course. The jumps are part of the galloping and the turning. You have to understand that, and he has to understand that. That's the safe way."

So we did it again, and I straightened my shoulders and put my heels down and paid better attention. I actually asked him to go a little bigger in his stride, though not faster, just to wake him up. This time he was smoother, and he changed his leads on the turns more quickly.

Rodney had now come into the ring, and Daddy and he shook hands. Rodney was about half the size of Daddy—well, not quite, but Daddy was clearly a cowboy and Rodney was clearly a jockey, and it was funny to watch them together. Daddy looked a little stiff and Rodney looked a little sassy. They all ran around putting the jumps up a hole. I did the course again, then they put the jumps up two holes.

Now Black George was interested. His ears were pricked, and he was taking hold of the bit, and he was tucking his hind end so that his back legs came under me. I could feel this, because it made him incredibly springy and comfortable. I made my circle and headed for the first jump, which was a green and white vertical with some painted boxes underneath the poles. Then there was a triple bar, which is three poles that rise from front to back, which looks scary but isn't because it always seems to draw the horse upward and over; then there was a chicken coop; and then a big crossbar, which doesn't look scary but is, because the horse sees and jumps over the high sides rather than the low middle. Then down over the in-and-out, vertical, and oxer; then back over the brush, this time with a pole across the top; and then the last vertical. They had set the gate in the middle of the last vertical, but Black George just flicked his ears and was over. We made our circle and came down to the trot. I looked over at the three of them. They were all smiling.

Rodney was the first to speak when I got to them. He said, "Are we shippin' this harse to Cheltn'm for a chaser, then? I've got a friend in Lambourn. . . ."

Jane said, "Much too good a horse for that, Rodney."

Daddy said, "You all right, Abby?"

I said, "Sure I am." But they were standing by one of the jumps I had jumped, and I noticed something about it for the first time—the top of the top pole was up to Rodney's chin and the middle of Daddy's chest, and that wasn't even the biggest jump. I said, "How high are these?"

Jane sniffed and opened her mouth to speak, but Rodney said, "Ah, goodness, four feet and a bit. They're hardly jumps, really. Yer lucky the harse notices 'em."

Jane said, "Rodney, don't you have some tack to clean?"

Rodney laughed and didn't move a muscle.

Daddy said, "Black George did it easy."

I nodded. But those words, *four feet*, made my heart pound in spite of everything. Once again, I was having two things happen at the same time. One thing was going around the course on Black George, easy and happy, and the other thing was knowing how big the course was and being scared through my whole body.

It was Rodney who noticed, or at least Rodney who said something. He said, "Give the girl a dram, miss. That's how we make up our minds to do the big courses, ya know."

Jane took her whip and smacked him, and said, "Go, please!"

He left, laughing the whole time, and she turned to Daddy and said, "Colonel Hawkins is crazy about Rodney, and he's a good horseman, but he goes too far at least once a day."

"Why is he crazy about the fellow?" said Daddy.

"Oh, Rodney makes him laugh. He takes him foxhunting, too. I guess he's good with the hounds. Drives me crazy, though. Sometimes I think it would be easier to do the work myself. So. Abby! Very good, dear. Do you want to do some more?"

Daddy looked at me. Right then, it was up to me, and there was part of me that had had enough (though I might not have said that if they hadn't told me how high the fences were), and there was part of me that was ready for another round. I sat there for a moment, then I said, "Don't you think he's had enough?"

Daddy said, "We can come back Saturday. For a short time."

And Jane said, "Let's do that, then," and that was the worst thing we could have done.

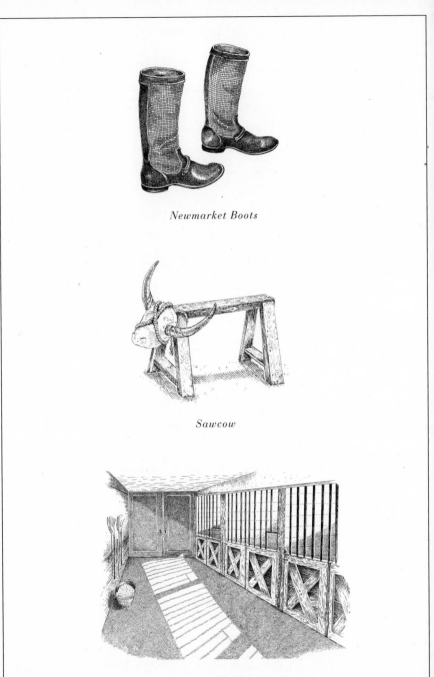

Newmarket Boots

Sawcow

Row of Stables

Chapter 11

I SHOULD HAVE FELT GOOD ABOUT OUR SESSION, AND I DID, IN A way. Daddy was proud of me, Jane gave me a little hug, and I knew that teasing was Rodney's way of being impressed—with me or the horse, but what was the difference? After we got home and were eating a late lunch, Daddy told Mom, "Well, Sarah, these two are getting better and better, thank the Lord."

"Of course they are," said Mom, but she gave me that look that said there was no "of course" about it. Then, while she was rinsing the lunch dishes, she started whistling. But everyone around me was feeling good—including Black George—and I wasn't. That number, four, was stuck in my head, and I knew we would do that again on Saturday. No big deal, just like Rodney said, at four feet, you're only starting to be a jumper. Even a regular working hunter jumps four-six.

After lunch, the weather got nice, so Mom and I took Sunshine and Jefferson up the hill, and then we took Lincoln and Sprinkles down to the crick. Daddy spent some time roping the sawcow from Happy's back, while I rode Effie in the arena, because a friend of Mr. Tacker's was going to come try Effie sometime soon, either tomorrow or next Monday. Mr. Hacker had bought two horses from us in the spring. The whole time we were riding in the arena, Rusty sat in the middle, keeping an eye on us. She was a funny dog. Sometimes, she came to the window and looked in, and when she saw Mom, she wagged her tail, which was long and bushy. But she knew she couldn't come inside, and she never asked to. Once, Mom said, "I don't think we've taken Rusty in as much as she's adopted us as her charges." That seemed about right. The funny thing was that late that afternoon, when Daddy went into town and Danny and Jake Morrisson showed up to shoe Sprinkles and Effie, Rusty walked right up to Danny and offered him her paw. She seemed to read Mom's mind, really.

After they were finished shoeing, Jake went into the house for a cup of coffee (and, I'm sure, to give Mom the latest on Danny), and Danny asked me to get out Jack and show him how he was doing. "He's doing fine," I said.

"Don't you want to get him out?"

"It's almost five o'clock and I'm bushed. I had him out yesterday."

"Let me get him out, then."

I shrugged. Danny gave me a look, but then he went and got the training halter and went to the gate of the gelding pasture. Jack didn't come to him, but Danny didn't care about that. He just walked into the pasture and stood quietly, and when the others came over, Jack came with them, and Danny patted him a few times along the side of his neck and stroked around his eye, and Jack dipped his head, and Danny slipped the halter on him. Then he turned and walked toward the gate. Jack walked right after him like a good boy.

I followed them to the pen.

Danny went into the center and sent Jack first to the left and then to the right, on the rope. Then he had him step back a few times, and then step under in both directions. Jack was good, but not perfect, because he was curious about Danny. He kept wanting to sniff his hands, then his chest, then his hair. Finally, Danny laughed, took off his hat, and bent his head, and Jack snuffled around his forehead and down over his ear.

I said, "Why does he want to do that?"

"Just being a baby, I guess."

Then they did some more stuff—picking up Jack's feet and dropping them, getting him to stand there quietly on a loose rein. Once he had been allowed to satisfy his curiosity about Danny, he behaved himself a little better.

Danny held the end of the rope out to me. It made me a little irritated. I shook my head.

"What is the matter with you?"

"I said I was tired."

"What did you do that made you so tired, then?"

"Well, we took Black George out to the stables and jumped him around everything. That was a day's work right there, but then we had to come home and do everyone else."

"Hmmp."

"What do you mean, *Hmmp?*"

"Can't I say *Hmmp* if I want to?"

I turned around and walked away, mostly because I was getting mad, and I didn't know why. I went in the barn, but I peeked out and watched Danny work Jack for a few more minutes, then walk him over to the gelding pasture and turn him out again. I stayed in the barn until I saw him drive away with Jake Morrisson. By then it was dark, and time to feed the horses, so I carried out the hay and checked the water.

When I went into the house, Mom was pulling a baked chicken out of the oven. Daddy drove up right then.

Over supper, we were all a little gloomy, I would have to say. I was mad because I was mad because I was mad. Didn't know why. Mom was always quiet after seeing Danny, and I was sure she had plenty to tell me about what he was doing, but she wouldn't tell me in front of Daddy, and Daddy knew Danny had been there and that Mom had a lot to tell, but he was too proud to ask her.

It had been a year now since Danny left after he and Daddy had a big fight at supper about whether Danny could go to a worldly movie (about space monsters). Daddy still expected him to come in remorse and ask to move back, but Danny was in the habit of living his own life, and Mom and I knew there was going to be no moving back, and therefore no apology.

Once, in the summer, he had even told Mom that moving out was the best thing he ever did in his whole life, and that night, Mom cried and Daddy marched around alternately saying, "Fine, good for him," and "The Lord knows what he is doing." The next day, which was Sunday, Daddy read a lesson about the Prodigal Son, and everyone at the service got dead quiet, and then, all of a sudden, Mr. Hazen started a long prayer, and frankly, I thought it was embarrassing.

But tonight, I didn't care about that. I was just mad. I went upstairs to my room after dinner and read an old book I liked, not about horses, a Nancy Drew where Nancy has to climb out of someone's chimney in order to save herself, and I fell asleep. But of course I knew why I was mad. I was mad at myself because I had been scared of those jumps, and I was still scared of them. Usually, like after the horse show, I liked to lie in bed with my eyes closed and imagine my way around the courses I had taken that day. If I really thought about it, it seemed like I could remember every stride and every jump and every turn, and it was both fun and comforting. The jumps in my mind were beautiful, and I could even see Black George's ears right in front of me, pointing at them. The feeling of the strides was smooth and easy, and more often than not, I got partway round the course and fell asleep.

But now that I knew those numbers, thinking of the course was like poison. It did put me to sleep, but a bad sleep, not a good sleep. All night long, the jumps looked huge and I was scared. When I got up in the morning, I had to give myself a little talking-to while I was brushing my teeth, about how I was being silly and it was no big deal and I must be crazy to think like this. The jumps were ones I had jumped. It was one thing to be scared of something I had not done, but it was another thing entirely to be afraid of something I actually had had no problem with. But this argument was depressing, too.

Finally, I made myself *not* think about those jumps, and

when it was time to ride Black George, I took him up the hill and rode him along the fence line, looking at the cows. The calves were big now—it's amazing how fast they grow—and they were jumping around and playing while the cows ate their hay.

All day Friday, I made myself not think about those jumps, or the fact that Saturday we were going to go back and do it again. At one point, Mom said, "You're awfully quiet," but I didn't say anything. Daddy was around, too, so she didn't tell me anything about Danny. In the afternoon, I tried to clean tack, but sitting there rubbing the leather gave me too much time to think, so I stopped that. Only when the man came to look at Sunshine did I sort of forget about it, and that was because the man fell off, and I had to run and catch Sunshine and then listen to Daddy trying to persuade the man that Sunshine hadn't "bucked" him off. And she hadn't. He had been holding tight to the rein, and she had put her head down, and he just fell over her shoulder. Of course we were glad to see him go, but there was not going to be a sale that weekend.

The thing about school was that you were always looking forward to the days off—they were going to be so great—but then sometimes they were very long and seemed to be sort of a waste of time. When I had finished my work on Friday, I couldn't believe that it was mid-afternoon and I was looking for a book to read and having no luck—all of my books were about horses, except for that Nancy Drew. Another irritating thing was that Stella had invited me and Gloria to spend the night Friday night, and I had turned her down without even asking Mom, just because I didn't think I would have the patience to sit around reading *Seventeen* and watching *The Man from U.N.C.L.E.*, which was a show they loved, all the time talking about Stella's diet, which had been very successful—she had lost twelve pounds and now was the same size as one of those *Seventeen* models, though how she actually knew that, I didn't understand.

Finally, I went to bed early. I thought it would be good to get to sleep, but it wasn't. I dreamt of Jack getting his hock caught in barbed wire, up by the calves and the cows, and in the dream, Mom kept saying, "How'd he get up there? I can't figure out how he got up there. Did he open the gate? Where are the other horses?" and I couldn't understand why she just kept talking about that when he had blood running down his leg.

So, Saturday morning we had all the horses fed and watered, and Black George loaded up by eight. I was yawning and yawning.

Daddy said, as we were pulling out of our driveway and turning onto the road, "The next show is in two weeks. Miss Slater is wondering if you might take half a day off Friday afternoon and go in a couple more classes."

I said I could do that.

"Will you have any tests that day?"

"I don't know. That's two weeks away!"

"I can't say that I like your tone." His own tone was low but meaningful, and I knew what it meant, but I said, anyway, "Well, what am I supposed to say? I can't predict the future!"

Daddy knew just how to drive a trailer—you do everything

smoothly, and you are always aware of the horse in the back—so, although he took a deep breath, he looked for a spot and then carefully pulled over, came to an easy halt, put the truck into neutral, and turned to me. He said, "Ruth Abigail, I am going to give you one chance to change your disrespectful attitude."

I sat there. Although he was not counting to ten out loud, I knew he was counting to ten in his head—I was, too. Around the time that we both got to eight, I said, "I'm sorry for being grumpy." This was just on the edge of being the right thing to say. I would have gotten in more trouble for saying "Sorry!" and he was looking for something like, "Daddy, I am really, really sorry I have been disrespectful and contrary." The edge was about all I could manage. He sighed and then, after a moment, looked in his sideview mirror, and pulled onto the road again. Back in the trailer, Black George whinnied. We had gone at least another five miles in silence when Daddy said, "Well, try to find out, and set it up ahead of time."

I said, "Okay." That was all we talked about on the way to the stables.

It was Saturday morning, so the stables were busy—lots of horses going in and out of the barns. It was a nice day, too—one of those days in autumn that are warm and sunny and calm, no fog, and the air bright, so trail rides were going out along with everything else. I saw Ellen running around, and I saw that girl Sophia Rosebury having a lesson with Colonel Hawkins. She was on the chestnut, who seemed to be doing fine today, but I didn't have time to watch because Jane came running up to us. She said, "Oh dear, the rings are jammed today! It seems like every single boarder suddenly remembered what they're spending to keep these animals. Look at Rodney!" She gestured toward the mounting block, where Rodney was holding a small black horse while a woman at least Daddy's age struggled to get on. Jane said, "The colonel has put Rodney absolutely in charge of Mrs. Jackson, who started out life as Miss Gould and has married railroads, airplanes, and hotels with equal lack of success. The colonel thinks Rodney can procure himself a sinecure."

I didn't ask what this was, because I could tell by the look on Daddy's face that it was something bad.

"Anyway," said Jane, "we will have to do the best we can under trying conditions."

We now had the tack on and adjusted. Black George's ears were forward, and as Daddy hoisted me up, Black George almost walked out from under me in his eagerness to get to the arena. But he was nice. He was like Alexis and Barbara weaving their way down the hall at school—excuse me; sorry; I don't even see you because I see my destination over there, but I am a nice horse, so I won't run over you or knock you down. We went on the light rein—we did not go to the farthest ring, where we had gone the first day (there was a group lesson in there) but to the one next to it, which was smallish but didn't have any trees in it. As I entered the gate, I heard Jane say, "Goodness, Ellen! Have you been following us? Hasn't your mother picked you up yet?"

"She's coming at noon."

I turned to look. Jane had her hands on her hips. "Noon! That's almost two and a half hours from now! What are you going to do until then?"

Ellen shrugged, but I could tell what she was going to do—be a pest. Daddy said, "Ellen, you stand here with me while Abby has her lesson." When she went over to him, he picked her up and sat her on the top board of the fence. I wandered to the end of the arena and then made a circle, shortening my reins and asking Black George to soften and gather himself together. He was so eager to get started that I hardly had to ask him. That's the way it is with a horse who has lots of energy—he feels ready to go and it's easy to organize him, but it's also easy to ask for too much and get a buck or some kicks.

But none of that with Black George—he picked up a courteous and willing trot, and we trotted all around the jumps, which Jane was arranging. When we passed Daddy, I heard him say to Ellen, "No, you have to be quiet and still. If you get excited, you can scare the horse. Don't you know that by now?"

I didn't hear what she said in reply.

Once Jane had the jumps set the way she liked them, she went to the far end of the ring and set a crossbar with a pole on either side. I was to trot over the first pole, canter the crossbar, and canter over the second pole, making sure to be in the exact center of every pole. I did this twice in each direction. Then she made the second pole into a small vertical, and I was to trot the first pole, canter the crossbar and the second pole. Finally, she made three jumps—crossbar, vertical, oxer, all one stride apart. Black George thought this was wonderful fun, trot, canter, jump, canter, jump, canter, jump, canter away—what could be easier, it was like doing three push-ups for him. Then she gave me my first course. There were no weird jumps in this arena—all standards and poles, white and natural-colored. The course made a big S curve, then a long loop, with the triple in-and-out second to last, just before a big oxer down the long side. The jumps weren't very high, so I sat up and made Black George gather his stride and go straight down the middle of every jump and very neatly around the corners. He was good, but bored by the jumps.

She put them up one hole, and we did it again.

I was having a good time, and it was funny to watch Daddy and Ellen. When she said, "Get me down!" he said, "Excuse me?" And she stared, or rather glared, at him for a second, then said, "Please, Mr. Lovitt, I would like to get down," so he took her down. I saw Jane smile at this.

But then she put the jumps up. It was like I had an eagle eye, even though I was having a good time, and when she put the jumps up, my temperature rose, too. I took off my sweat-shirt. This time, I only barely remembered the way around. It was like my knowing the fact that she had put the jumps up got in the way of the course, literally—I kept seeing in my mind that the poles were moving and I couldn't remember anything else. But I only missed one jump—I cantered right past the one before the in-and-out, a white vertical. When I finished the course, she said, "That's okay, you can get that one the next time around."

And she put the jumps up.

Daddy was busy talking to Ellen—I couldn't hear what he was saying. Jane was walking toward me, brushing her hands off and smiling. The trees at one side of the ring were rustling, and some horse and rider were standing outside of the ring, watching us. I said, "How high are they?" and without really thinking about it, Jane said, "Oh, four feet, something like that," and it was like I couldn't think anymore. I made a noise of some kind, maybe a groan, and Jane looked up at me. She said, "These are easy for him. You've done this before. Now, just the same—"

"I can't do it."

"Sure you can. You did do it. More than once."

"I don't care. I can't do it."

"Abby! Don't be—"

I knew she wanted to say "silly," but she didn't. Instead, she stood there looking at me, thinking about what to do. Daddy came into where we were standing. Jane said, "She doesn't want to go any higher. It's no problem for the horse, of course, but . . ."

Daddy pushed his cowboy hat back on his head and looked up at me. He was about to say something when a voice called out, "I'll ride him."

We all looked around. There, by the gate, was Sophia Rosebury, and she was already in the process of springing off her chestnut. She was the person on a horse that I had seen standing there. I didn't say anything because I knew Daddy would shake his head no, and then we would have to figure something else out—maybe Jane would get on Black George— but Daddy didn't shake his head no. He looked at Jane, who looked at him, and said, "Well, this is as good a time as any."

As good a time as any for what?

Sophia ran up the stirrups on her saddle and brought the reins over her horse's head, and led him into the arena. She had on Newmarket boots, which were boots with rubber feet and canvas legs. Lots of people had them for training, but you couldn't wear them in a show. When she got closer, I saw that hers did not have rubber feet; they had regular leather feet, which meant they were custom-made.

Daddy said, "I suppose that's true."

I suppose what's true?

Sophia and her horse got closer, and then off in the distance, I saw Colonel Hawkins coming in our direction at a fast walk. I thought he would stop her for sure, but when he got to the gate, he said, "Ready?"

Ready for what?

Jane shrugged and said, "Well, he's warmed up. Might as well."

Daddy glanced at me and said, "Well, let's try it. Abby, why don't you get down and—"

"Get down off Black George?"

"You heard me."

And I did. And if I hadn't already gotten in trouble for being sassy that morning, I might have said something or just sat there, but I had, so I didn't. I dismounted—a little slowly, I admit—and traded reins with Sophia. I held the chestnut, and she mounted Black George from the ground. She had incredibly long, thin legs, and she just put her foot up there and bounced on. When she picked up the reins, Black George pricked his ears and headed to the rail without a backward glance. Well, a horse can make a backward glance without turning his head, but not Black George, not this time. He was set to jump, and he didn't care if it was me on his back or Sophia. In the meantime, the chestnut sneezed all over my shoulder.

Sophia knew the course, I suppose from watching—she had been going to shows for a long time, so maybe she was fast about learning courses. She began her trot circle, went up into the canter, galloped down around the S curve, then around the loop, slowing down a bit for the triple in-and-out, and then sitting up and asking for a bigger stride on the last fence. For me, it was amazing to see Black George jump because, as I realized while watching them, I never had before—I had always been the one riding. Sophia was a good rider—her form was perfect over every fence, her back straight, her heels down, her eyes looking where she was going, and her hands always alongside his black neck, the reins straight like taut threads between her hands and his mouth. Yes, she looked like a stick figure, but it was the sort of stick figure you draw to show what the right way to do something is. Over each jump, her braids flopped on her back.

But really, for me, the one to watch was Black George. I could see why Jane and Daddy were surprised I was scared, because he just bent his knees and went over the jump. And if you couldn't tell by his form that it was easy and he was having a good time, then you could tell by the look on his face, which was perfectly calm. Horses have all kinds of looks on their faces as they are going to the jump—I had seen that at shows. With some, their eyes are wide and their ears are up and their nostrils are flared, and maybe they will refuse. Others look dull and others look determined, and others even look tricky—Sophia's chestnut, who was breathing down the back of my neck right then, looked tricky that time, which meant no expression on his face and then his eyes narrowed and he was out of there.

I saw one horse who jumped all the jumps but was grinding his bit the whole time. Black George had the look of a horse who was taking care of his job and who liked his job. Just watching him made that skittery feeling of "four" and "feet" go away.

Then Sophia turned him in a circle and brought him down to the trot. She trotted over to us, did her leg-over-the-neck dismount while Ellen was clapping and shouting "Hurray." Then Sophia said to Colonel Hawkins, "Yeah, I like him." She threw him the reins. She didn't say a word to me when I handed her the reins of the chestnut gelding, nor did she give the gelding a pat or say hi to him. She just said to the colonel, "I'm taking this one to be put away. I'll get on the mare." And off they went.

The colonel had better manners, at least. He shook Daddy's hand, then came over to me and said, "Thank you, Abigail, for letting us try your horse. You've done an excellent job with him." Then he patted me on the head and handed me the reins, but only after giving Black George another piece of sugar. I didn't like being patted on the head, and I didn't like being called Abigail. I threw my arms around Black George's neck and put my face against his coat. He smelled good—sweaty but clean and healthy. Then I walked him over to the fence, stood him up beside it, and got on the fence to mount. It felt good to be on his back. I settled myself in the saddle and then leaned down and patted him on the neck. I told him what a good boy he was, all the time, every day, and then I walked him over to Jane and Daddy.

I said, "That was good. I learned something from that. Shall we try a different course?"

Jane said, "Oh, I think he's had enough for today."

Daddy said, "What did you learn?"

"I learned that it really is not a problem for him, whatever the numbers are."

The two of them smiled. Jane said, "I'm so glad you realize—"

I interrupted her. I said, "I learned that if you stop when you're scared, like I did the other day, then you'll be scared until you start again, and maybe after you start again."

Daddy smiled, and Jane said, "Well, that *is* a good lesson. I never really thought of it that way, but of course it's true."

"So, I want to go again."

Daddy and Jane looked at each other, and there was a long, quiet moment, quiet except for, of course, all the sounds from the barn and the rings and the rustling trees and the birds, but quiet to me. And then Daddy said, "Yes, Abby, you learned some very good lessons, but the fact is, he's had plenty, and I don't think it would be good for him to go around again."

Jane said, "He's a valuable horse. Best not take any chances."

Of course, then I knew what was coming next. I was amazed I had been so dumb. Sooner or later—and if Daddy had his way, sooner—my horse was going to be Sophia Rosebury's horse, and it didn't matter if she ever patted him or gave him a treat or even remembered his name (which she would certainly change, anyway). Daddy squeezed me around the shoulders and we started walking back toward the truck and trailer, me leading Black George, and Daddy and Jane walking a little ahead of us. He had a beautiful face, Black George, with a quiet eye and quick ears—he flicked them back and forth in order to keep track of what was going on, but nothing worried him. His best feature was his mouth—smooth, long lips, just relaxed, because he didn't wrinkle them all the time. As we walked, I stroked his nose.

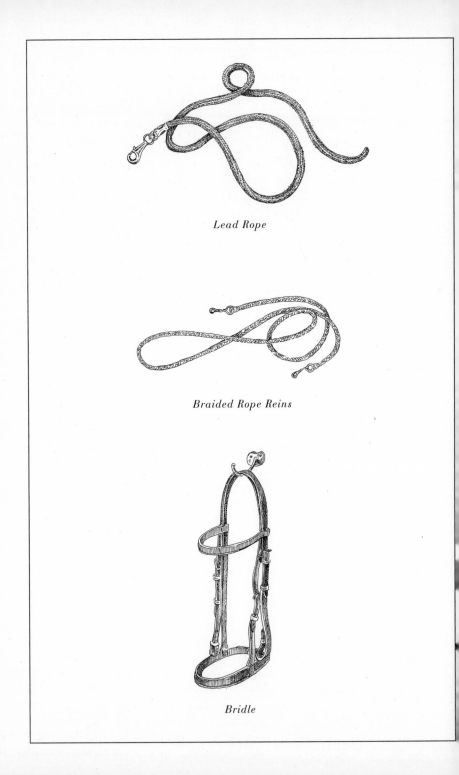

Lead Rope

Braided Rope Reins

Bridle

Chapter 12

IT WAS COLONEL HAWKINS'S VET, SOMEONE WE DIDN'T KNOW, who came out to inspect Black George. Just having a vet look at the horse was a sign of how much they thought of him. When we sold Melinda Aniston the gray pony, all they did was look him over very carefully, flex his joints, trot him out, and let us know that if something turned up in the first week or two that showed we'd misrepresented him (given him some kind of drug, really), we would get him back and return the money. People bought and sold horses all the time, and having a vet go over every one of them would be very time-consuming. When Daddy went to Oklahoma and bought horses, he went over them inch by inch himself and prayed for guidance, but if he needed a vet to find out something about a horse, then that was a horse he didn't want, anyway.

The vet even brought an assistant to hold the horse and trot him out and to run to the truck and get this and that. They came at the end of the day, and I had work to do, but while I was riding Jefferson and then after I got on Happy, I could see them going over him. Daddy did things in the barn while they worked, and then I could see the assistant hand Daddy the lead rope, thank him, and get in the vet's truck. We would hear, not from the vet himself but from Colonel Hawkins.

According to Mom and Daddy, it was not my job to know what sort of price we might get for Black George, but according to me, it was my job to keep my ears open, even if I didn't ask any questions. And keep my window open, if the weather wasn't too cold. At first, I couldn't understand why they were being so secretive—Daddy often talked about how he bought a horse for four hundred dollars and sold her for eight hundred, and her keep over the months had cost such and such and every shoeing was six dollars, but I decided that what was really going on was that they didn't dare say the amount aloud. Twice when I passed through the kitchen, I heard them lower their voices as they said the word *ten*. I guessed that they were asking for ten thousand dollars.

Ten thousand dollars was an unbelievable amount of money. I knew we had sold the pony for thirty-five hundred, because Daddy had not been able to contain himself after he made the deal and had burst out with that on the way home from the stable. Other than that, I didn't know much except that when they wondered whether Jack's stud fee was more than they could afford, if it turned out that we had to pay to keep him, they started shaking their heads at a thousand dollars. A pair of good riding boots was forty-five dollars, and when Mom had stopped with me once at a car dealer's and asked the price of one of the cars, it was two thousand. Danny, we heard, had paid five hundred for his, and it was still running. So I had no way of knowing how much money ten thousand dollars was, except that Daddy and Mom never said the words above a whisper.

Wednesday night, when I was in my room doing homework, the phone rang and Daddy answered it and talked for a long time, as long as he would to Uncle Luke if he called, but he didn't raise his voice or invoke the name of the Lord, so it couldn't be Uncle Luke. I even went out into the hall to see if I could hear something, but Daddy was being so polite that I couldn't make out a word. Every whisper was a reminder to me that I should be happy rather than sad. We had done the thing that every horse trader wants to do—find the diamond lying by the side of the road, pick it up when no one else sees it, polish it. I had shown off the diamond and gotten prizes and praise. Now it looked like other people, people who knew the business, agreed that the diamond was a diamond and not just another rhinestone.

I wasn't supposed to feel that they were stealing my diamond, but I did. I'd been riding Black George all these months—almost a year now—and he had been so easy and agreeable and comfortable and willing that I had forgotten there would be an end to it. Every horse feels different. It's like looking at people's faces—each face is itself, and you can always tell them apart. Horses' faces don't look as different as people's faces do—that was the reason no one could be sure whether Pearl was Alabama Lady or not. But every horse was unique to ride, and Black George, I thought, was uniquely good. And the worst thing about it was that I would not be able to remember how he felt after a while—there's nothing like a photograph to remind your body how a certain horse's canter flowed along or exactly the way a certain horse's jump lifted you up and over. And the rest of it was fun, too—going to lessons with Jane, going to the show. I realized that it's one thing to know that something won't last and quite another to find out that it's over.

And then, on Thursday, Barbara Goldman came up to me after lunch, while Stella and Gloria were in the girls' bathroom and I was rearranging my schoolbag.

She said, "Abby, I wondered how you did on the *Julius Caesar* test."

"I got an A, which is thanks to you."

"Leslie, Maria, and Alexis got As, too."

"What about you?"

Barbara grinned. "I would have gotten an A if I'd bothered to turn the test sheet over and answer all the questions."

"You're kidding! You were the one who told us all the answers."

Barbara shrugged. "I was thinking about something else, I guess. Listen, you want to spend the night tomorrow night? We aren't doing anything much, but we thought it would be fun. You did so great as Antony."

How could you turn down an invitation to spend the night at the Goldmans'? I didn't even say I would ask Mom; I just said, "Yes." Barbara said, "Well, great! Bring your clothes in the morning, and we'll just go home from school on our bus, and your mom can pick you up Saturday."

I said, "I'll probably have to go home early to start my riding."

"But you have to stay for breakfast, because Saturday we have bagels and lox, with cream cheese, and they're so good."

I said, "What's that?"

Now Barbara really laughed but said, "A bagel is like a roll, but they boil it before they bake it. We always have the poppy seed kind. And lox is smoked salmon."

I couldn't imagine what she was talking about.

When I got home, both the car and the truck were gone, and Rusty was taking care of things, or that's what it seemed like. As soon as I got off the bus, she came down to the gate and sat right in the middle of the driveway while I opened it, then she approached me, wagging her tail slowly from side to side, and accompanied me up to the house, where she sat down on the porch and watched me go in.

When I came out after changing my clothes, she walked with me to the gelding pasture, where I patted Jack and Black George on their noses, then she sat there. It was only when I headed for the barn that she whined. I had never heard her whine before, and she had a strange whine, low rather than high, but not at all like a growl. The closer I got to the barn, the more she whined, and then she barked. Now I got that she was trying to tell me something, so I stood there for a moment and looked around. It was then that I saw that the mares had somehow turned over their water trough. They were all standing near it, and when Rusty barked, they looked at us. Or at me. I went and filled the water trough.

When Mom and Daddy and I were talking about this at supper, we could not decide what was going on. The water trough had been dumped since morning, because the ground around it was almost dry, so the mares were pretty thirsty, and in fact, they did all take big drinks after I filled it. But they were not dehydrated—Daddy pinched the skin on each of their necks right in front of their shoulders when he got home—if the pinch stays pinched, then the horse is dehydrated, and the longer it stays pinched, the more you have to worry. None of their pinches stayed pinched. They might have gone down to the crick for a drink, but even with the rain we had had, the crick was just a trickle.

The real question was, how did Rusty know?

Mom said, "Well, look at her! It's her job to know. That's what *she* thinks."

Daddy said, "Horses do not talk to dogs!"

"Horses don't have to talk to communicate. If they want to eat, they nose their food tubs. If they want to get out, they kick the door of the stall."

Daddy said, "Remember a couple of years ago? One of the geldings got a quarter crack and had to stay in that pen we had then, for a month? Danny dumped his water bucket one day and forgot to fill it, and the next day, when I was walking past the stall, he went over to his bucket and stood there nodding his head until I checked it."

I said, "And you're the one who always says it has to be the carrot or the stick or they don't understand."

Mom said, "Rusty probably saw them knock over the trough. She sees everything."

Daddy said, "So she made the connection between dumping the trough and something being wrong?"

Mom smiled. "It's you who always says that animals were made to serve man, and now you don't believe your own eyes."

I thought she had him there.

It wasn't until bedtime that I remembered about the Goldmans. But Mom said yes, they seemed to be very nice people, and she gave me a little overnight bag for my clothes. She also said, "I think it's good for you to get away for a night, I really do," and she kissed me on the forehead, though she had to reach up to do it. No one said a word about Black George.

Of course I had to tell Gloria and Stella that I was spending the night at the Goldmans'. Stella exclaimed, "Are they even your friends?" and I could see that Gloria was hurt that I would go there when I hadn't come to her house the week before. I said, "Well, we had fun doing the play. I don't know why they asked me."

"No one ever knows why they do anything. I mean, they practice music for hours. You'll probably have to listen to that. They're very artsy. My mom said they're from New York." Stella said this as though it meant something important.

Things got all quiet.

I said, "Well, I have more free time now, because that horse I was riding so much might be sold." I glanced at Gloria as if this were a job that I was about to be relieved of, and she smiled and said, "Well, that's good." I nodded. And maybe it was, in a way.

But Mom was right—going to the Goldmans' was a complete break from my entire life. Riding to their house on the bus was fun enough—Alexis and I sat in the front seat and Barbara sat right behind us, leaning forward with her hand on the back of our seat the whole time. They talked about the same things we all did—teachers, classes, homework, boys— but they talked about them in a different way, as if they were interesting rather than boring and offensive. Between them, they had a lot of teachers, because they took eighth-grade classes and ninth-grade classes, and because they were "separated" for most of their classes.

"Mom did that," said Alexis, "because until we were in second grade, we refused to say who we were, so the teachers were always calling us by each other's names. We thought that was really funny. I would go for a whole day saying I was Barbara, and then the next day, a teacher would ask Barbara something and she would not know it!"

"We used to dress alike," said Barbara, "but that made it worse, so Mom put us in different outfits."

"So we just went into the girls' bathroom and switched clothes if we felt like it."

"They had us in the principal's office all the time."

Alexis shook her head. "Mom was going out of her mind."

"Well, that's what she told us. But you couldn't tell."

"She already is out of her mind!" They laughed.

Barbara said, "So they figured out which teachers could deal with us and sort of divvied us up between them, and even though we don't make any trouble anymore, they still do that."

"It's school district policy with all twins now."

Barbara pursed her lips in a merry way. "We were such troublemakers!" They laughed again. I laughed, too.

I said, "Do you ever dress alike now?" It was true that it was hard to tell them apart, but sitting with them, I could—Barbara's eyes were bluer, and Alexis had slightly fuller cheeks.

"Well," said Alexis, "we are mirror twins. If those teachers had bothered to look, they would have seen that I'm right-handed and Barbie's left-handed, and even though we've practiced, we can't switch."

"Our cousin Leo says you can change your whole personality if you practice writing with your wrong hand, but even though we've tried, we can't do it."

I said, "Kyle Gonzalez does that, too."

The twins looked at each other and said, "Boys are from another world." They nodded together.

Listening to them almost made you want to be a twin.

They didn't have horses to ride when they got home, but they did have music to play, just as Stella had predicted, so while they practiced for an hour, I sat in the kitchen with Mrs. Goldman and her sister, Mrs. Marx, and their cousin, Leah Marx. Leah was a senior in high school, and the question was whether she should apply for early admission to Stanford or to Berkeley. I didn't know what they were talking about. Finally, Leah turned to me and said, "Your brother, Danny, what's he doing now? I always thought he was cute."

"He's working for a horseshoer."

"He's not in school at all?" said Mrs. Marx.

"He's gainfully employed!" said Mrs. Goldman. "Abby here is a superb equestrienne. She rides every day."

"Do you!" said Mrs. Marx. "I always wanted to do that. I thought I would have talent."

"You couldn't even skip rope," said Mrs. Goldman.

"I couldn't do doubles."

"I could do doubles all day," said Mrs. Goldman.

"Once, she skipped rope for three hours straight, from after school until dark. It took ten girls in shifts to twirl the ropes, and then she came home and passed out."

"I'm sure it was a world's record," said Mrs. Goldman.

"I thought you were dead."

"That's what she told our mother," said Mrs. Goldman.

"She didn't react as if she cared much."

"Only because she never believed a word you said, anyway!"

Mrs. Goldman slapped Mrs. Marx on the shoulder, and the two of them began to laugh.

I said, "Are you twins, too?"

"Not by a long shot," said Mrs. Goldman. "I'm two years older, but thank you for not noticing the difference."

"It's much more visible in stronger light," said Mrs. Marx.

"Abby, have a Coke," said Mrs. Goldman. "You must be thirsty."

She went to the refrigerator and took out a Coke, popped the cap, and gave it to me with a glass. Then she said, "You don't want ice, do you? I like it full strength myself."

I had never heard grown-ups talk this way.

For supper, there was a big crowd—the four Goldmans; three Marxes (Leah's brother was already at college, at UCLA); a friend of Mr. Goldman's who came home with him, named

Mr. Wiggins; the next-door neighbor, who was an old lady named Mrs. Allen ("She eats with us almost every night," said Barbara. "All of her family is in Arizona now"); and me. We had a pile of noodles with a spicy red sauce called "linguini with puttanesca sauce" and big leaves of lettuce with cubes of toasted bread and cheese. Mr. Goldman made the dressing at the table by mashing little fish with oil and some egg and some other things. Barbara said, "Do you like Caesar salad?"

I said, "I have no idea." I did what Mom always told me to do and ate a little of everything. The bread and butter was good. There was no grace and everyone at the table talked the whole time. The grown-ups drank wine. Mrs. Allen spilled her water, and Mrs. Goldman kept talking while she was cleaning it up, and then, after the food was all gone, everyone sat at the table and kept talking. Leah was the quiet one, but she was busy—she kept picking up the napkins (cloth) and folding them in the shapes of animals, then she would set them on the table in various positions and make them move as if they were talking to one another. She saw me watching her, and we kept laughing. She was not blond, like the Goldman twins, but about my size and with dark, curly hair. I wondered how well she had known Danny, but I didn't ask her.

After dinner, we broke into two teams and played a game called "Adverbs" in the big living room where we had done the play. Alexis and I were on one team, and Barbie and Leah were on the other. Even Mrs. Allen played. When one of your team members left the room, the rest of you decided on an adverb for that person to act out when he or she came back, and then it was the job of the other team to guess the adverb he or she was acting out. The first person to leave was Mr. Goldman, who was on the other team. When he came back, they whispered the word to him, and then he got down on his hands and knees and began dragging himself across the floor, putting his hand to his brow and looking around from time to time, or collapsing on the carpet. Our team kept calling out words, and finally Mrs. Marx shouted, "Desperately." That was the word.

Then it was our turn. Alexis left, and we consulted one another (or they did—I didn't say anything). When she came back, Mr. Wiggins (but everyone called him "Bill") whispered the word *idly* to her. She carried a chair to the middle of the room, between the two teams, and sat down half turned in the seat, with her right arm over the back of the chair. Then she yawned, then she sighed, then she began to stare out the window and twist a lock of hair between her fingers. After only three or four minutes, Barbie shouted, "Idly!" Then they made a rule that Barbie couldn't guess when it was Alexis's turn and vice versa. The next word was *monstrously*, which was played by Leah. First she tromped around with her shoulders up and her chin out while everyone came up with variations on *tall-ly*, then she went over to Mr. Goldman and pretended to strangle him, at which point Bill guessed, "Monstrously."

And so I had to go to the bathroom, and I couldn't avoid being the next person. Their guest bathroom was nice, and I stayed there for a while, but I had to come back, and when I sat down on the couch, Alexis whispered "tentatively" in my ear. I thought for a minute. *Tentatively* was a word I had read but had never heard anyone use. I knew what it meant, though. I decided not to go out into the middle of the room—that wouldn't be tentative enough. I closed my eyes and put my hands in front of my face for a moment, then I opened my eyes and peeked between my hands. Mrs. Goldman said, "Oh, she's doing it."

"Shyly?" said Barbie.

I put my hands down, then waited a second, then put my foot out and brought it back. Then I peered around Alexis, but just for a bit. I put my hand in front of my mouth. I opened my mouth as if I were going to say something, then closed it. I could feel myself fill up with being tentative—thinking I might try something, and almost daring to do so, but not quite. Was "tentatively" about not wanting to or not daring to? Both, I decided. I half stood up, but sat down again, shook my head, but only a little.

The other team was calling out words—*hopefully, nervously, shyly* again, *anxiously*—and my team was laughing. I almost laughed myself, because I couldn't help it, then I realized that I could make my laugh "tentative," so I giggled, then covered my mouth and lowered my eyes. Mrs. Goldman shouted, "Tentatively!" and everyone said, "Yes! Yes! That's it!"

We played a lot of rounds—when Barbie was acting, Alexis whispered words in my ear that I called out, but she wasn't right any more often than anyone else was. I did *woodenly* (by acting like a tree, then a carpenter hammering), *nosily* (by going over to where the other team was sitting and sniffing them, which made everyone laugh), and *juicily* (by pretending to squeeze fruit and being surprised at how wet I got).

The best word Barbie did was *comically*, and for Alexis it was *automatically*. But the best word of the night was when Mr.

Goldman did *apoplectically*. First, he pretended to be so angry that all of us fell silent because he did such a good job that he made us a little afraid of him, and then, when we kept shouting variations on *angrily*, he made a face, grabbed his throat and fell down, and then jerked around on the ground. Because no one could guess, he went on for three or four minutes, getting wilder and wilder, which made it hard. At that point, Mrs. Marx shouted, "Apoplectically," and Mr. Marx said, "Yes, apoplexy was originally a stroke!" We gave him a round of applause, and he said, "Well, finally! I was killing myself!" and started to laugh.

We staggered up to bed about midnight. They had set up a cot in Barbie and Alexis's room, but they told me to sleep in the lower bunk, because that was more comfortable, and so I got out my pajamas. The girls also had their own bathroom, which they had painted themselves with trees and animals, mostly cats and birds, and when we had finished brushing our teeth, I stayed in there a minute to look around. I thought the rooster and the bluebird were the best, and the black cat sitting on a white step, but I couldn't tell if just one of the twins had painted those, because there were no initials or anything. But really, they were all good.

By the time I got into the room, all the lights but the night-light were off, and Barbie and Alexis were in bed and seemed to be asleep. Only when I had gotten into my bunk did anyone say anything, and that was Alexis, in the cot, who sounded half asleep when she said, "Night night."

I fell asleep right away, too. My head was full of adverbs and faces, and laughing, and the flat darkness, across the living room, of that big window that looked out over the valley. The twins' room had lots of windows, too, and I could hear an owl hoot as I fell asleep. My head was so full that I didn't think of Mom or Daddy or Black George at all, and I forgot my nighttime prayer (though I remembered that and said it when I woke up for a moment in the night). I did not have any dreams.

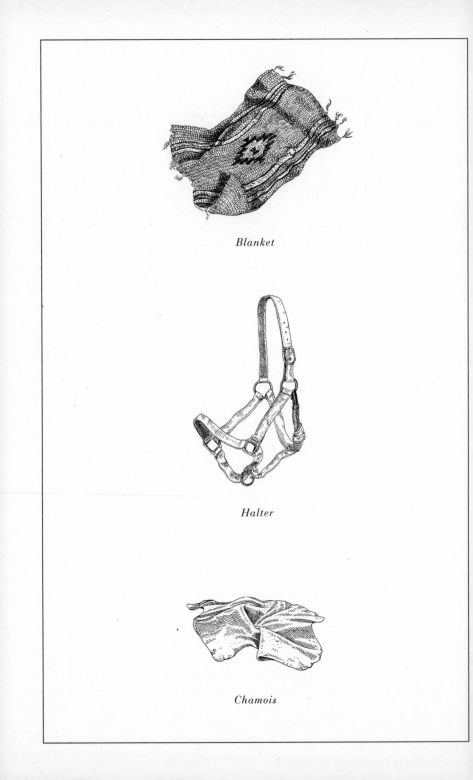

Blanket

Halter

Chamois

Chapter 13

A BAGEL TURNED OUT TO BE A ROUND ROLL, LIKE A DOUGHNUT, but hard and not sweet. Poppy seeds turned out to be tiny black, crunchy seeds that were sprinkled on top of the bagel. Mrs. Goldman had a special wooden block that she set the bagel in. She cut it in two, toasted it, and spread it with cream cheese, then laid flat orange slices of lox on it. Lox was fish, and sort of slimy, but also very salty, and along with some sliced pineapple and melon, that was breakfast. Alexis and Barbie drank coffee, just like their parents.

Mom showed up while we were still eating, and they had her come in and sit down and have a cup of coffee. Mom said, "We really have to . . . ," but she sat down and received her cup, poured in the (real) cream, and took a spoonful of sugar.

"Abby has been so much fun," said Mrs. Goldman. "We played Adverbs last night for the first time in years, and Abby made us all laugh when she did *nosily*."

I said, "Mr. Goldman was the funniest."

"Oh my goodness," said Mrs. Goldman. "I'd forgotten how deeply he gets into every adverb. I am truly glad no one asked him for *mortally*!"

"How would you do that one?" said Alexis.

"I don't think it's really an adverb," said Barbie. "I think it's an adjective, like *decidedly*."

The twins stuck their tongues out at each other.

Mrs. Goldman passed the plate of bagels to Mom and said, "These are good bagels. I went out for them early this morning." Mom hesitated, then took half of one of the split ones. Mrs. Goldman handed her a plate, and Alexis passed her the cream cheese. She spread some on and took a bite, then said, "Hmm. That is good."

"These are the real thing—just a little chewy. Hard to find in California, at least around here. But there's one place."

Barbie said to her, "The melon is good, too," and passed her the melon. Mom took two slices and set them on her plate. The lox was gone. It was interesting to see Mom with the Goldmans, because she was pretty shy about strangers. I knew that when she first sat down, she was feeling out of place and ready to get out of there as soon as possible, but everyone was so friendly that they seemed not to notice that she didn't have much to say, just went on with what they were already doing.

Mrs. Goldman said, "What lessons do you girls have today?"

"Banjo," said Barbie.

"Banjo!" said Mrs. Goldman. "How did that happen?"

"I signed up behind your back. I want to branch out."

"How much is it?" said Mrs. Goldman, but she didn't seem angry, or even really surprised.

"It's free. I'm trading for violin with Horton Jenkins. He thinks if he can play the fiddle, his band will be more flexible."

"I thought they had a fiddle player," said Alexis.

"They do, but he wants to have two fiddles on some songs."

"Why doesn't their fiddle player teach him?"

"Because I'm the one who wants to play the banjo."

Mom said, "My brother plays the banjo, back in Oklahoma."

I knew this.

"Oh!" exclaimed Barbie. "Is he good?"

"He's fast. I stopped trying to keep up with him when I was about Abby's age."

"What did you play?" asked Alexis.

"We had an old mandolin," said Mom.

I didn't know this.

"I sang a little, too."

It was true that when we were in church, Mom knew all the songs, and she was great on the high parts.

"Do you play anything, Abby? We could have a band."

I shook my head.

Mom said, "Abby has a good voice, though."

Alexis and Barbie turned toward me at the same time, and Mrs. Marx said, "You girls have plenty going on without starting a band."

"Just sing one thing," said Alexis. "One verse of one song."

Silence all around the room. Mom was smiling at me. She

knew we were well practiced, from church. I bit my lips for a moment, then sang, "Old Stewball was a racehorse, and I wish he were mine. He never drank water, he always drank wine. His bridle was silver, and his mane it was gold—"

Mom came in on the high harmony, "And the worth of his saddle has never been told."

Now Alexis and Barbie came in, too. Barbie was the low one, and Alexis was in my range, but doing a sort of counterpoint: "Well, the fairgrounds were crowded, Old Stewball was there, but the betting was heavy, on the bay and the mare."

Now we fell silent, and Mom sang, "Well, I bet on the gray mare, and I bet on the bay."

Then we all chimed in, "If I'd a bet on Old Stewball, I'd be a free man today!"

Then we laughed.

Alexis said, "That's a Peter, Paul, and Mary song. I love that song."

"Very good! Very good!" exclaimed Mrs. Goldman, "Don't sing any more or I'll be driving this band around day and night." But she kept clapping.

Mom was grinning. When we left, Mrs. Goldman gave her a little kiss on the cheek and said, "Drop by anytime!"

After we were in the car, Mom said, "Well, you must have had fun."

Before I realized what I was saying, it popped out: "I never knew you could have that much fun."

There was a pause, and then she said, "They do seem nice."

At home, there was plenty to do, because the Roseburys had bought Black George and they were going to pick him up late that afternoon. They would have preferred Sunday, but that was out. It wasn't that he needed cleaning, it was that the whole place needed cleaning, because Colonel Hawkins, Mr. Rosebury, and Sophia were all coming, and however the place looked to us, there was always the chance that it could look like a dump to them.

"Not a dump," said Daddy, "but a working ranch rather than a showplace."

"That's bad enough," said Mom. She had already mopped the kitchen floor and cleaned the stove in case they accepted her invitation for a cup of tea. Daddy had swept the barn and straightened all the racks: saddles and bridles and halters and lead ropes and blankets and pictures—you name it, it was wound up, folded, hanging straight, put away. Mom had even brushed Rusty. Dad had replaced two boards on the fence of the gelding pasture that the horses had chewed, and all in all we were acting way more impressed by Sophia than I wanted to, but it did come out—Daddy let it slip—that the Roseburys were paying "at least ten thousand dollars" for Black George.

"What do you mean, 'at least'?"

"I mean that we get it all. Normally, there would be commissions to Jane and maybe Colonel Hawkins, and they would come out of our money, but there's none of that."

The good thing was that in my two days and one night at the Goldmans' house, I had gotten used to it, so when I gave Black George one last brushing, all over, from ears to tail, and then rubbed him down with the chamois, I felt a little separated from him, as if he had already gone and only his ghost were here. I suppose that's what Daddy meant when he talked about accepting the will of the Lord—you have had some feelings, and you knew you had them, but you put them in a box and you put the box away. I guess that was what everyone meant by growing up, too.

In the end, though, it was Colonel Hawkins and Rodney who showed up. Sophia and her father were "otherwise detained" and couldn't make it. The two men didn't come into the house for tea, but they did look around. They even asked if they could walk over to the gelding pasture and the mare pasture and have a look at the horses—"You needn't get them out, but Jane speaks so highly . . ." So they strolled over to the fence and looked at everyone. I was sorry Lester was gone— Lincoln and Jefferson looked like what they were, regular horses who would work for a living at regular jobs. Rodney said, "Is that the colt?"

And Daddy said, "Yes, that's Abby's colt."

Of the mares, Colonel Hawkins liked Happy. He said she was "athletic-looking."

"Born cow horse," said Daddy. "Bossy as the day is long."

Colonel Hawkins laughed.

I could see that they knew they were getting our best horse, and no one else even came close.

They looked Black George over, and Rodney bandaged his legs for the trip. They had brought their own light blanket, green with a rose embroidered on it and *ROR* in curly letters beneath that. I guessed that stood for "Something Something Rosebury." Leather halter, leather lead line with a brass chain between the hook and the leather. Beautiful trailer, brand-new white truck. The rose and the *ROR* were painted on the trailer, too. Sure enough, Black George was going to live like a king.

I kissed him on the cheek and patted him on the neck, and Rodney loaded him into the trailer and lifted up the ramp, then he got into the passenger's side of the truck. The colonel and Rodney were already talking to each other by the time they pulled away. They didn't even wave good-bye.

On Monday, Gloria and Stella were a little stiff with me. When I said to Stella, "Oh, those are nice loafers," she said, "Well, they aren't Bass Weejuns." Then I remembered that Alexis wore Bass Weejuns. When I asked Gloria what she did over the weekend, she said, "I can't really remember." But she thawed out by lunchtime and wanted to know all about the Adverbs game. I also told her about the bathroom. She said, "Their mom let them do that?"

"Yeah. Basically, they do whatever they want to."

Gloria thought for a moment and said, "Yes, they do. I see that." She sighed, then suggested, "Well, maybe they'll come to a bad end." We laughed. At first, I felt sorry about laughing at Alexis and Barbara, and then I thought, well, they would laugh at that, too.

As for Alexis and Barbara, they were friendly, but they weren't my new best friends or anything. They still bustled down the hall in the morning rather than huddle with other kids around their lockers. They still sat at their own table for lunch and didn't invite others to sit there, though they were perfectly nice if anyone did. In fact, one of the amazing things about the Goldman twins was that they didn't change—they were always themselves. Now that I'd been to their house, I saw that that was the way the whole Goldman family was.

Maybe if you always did what you wanted to do, then you always were who you wanted to be.

At home, I missed Black George. There was a big hole in the gelding pasture, and it was in the shape of Black George. With Lester gone, too, there were only Jefferson and Lincoln and Jack. Daddy also thought he had a buyer for Sprinkles, and maybe one for Effie, so with all this new money, he was planning to go back to Oklahoma before the winter set in and see what he could find. He said, "Colonel Hawkins is right—there are plenty of good horses back there if you have a good eye and can spend the time looking for them."

"Black Georges are pretty few and far between," said Mom, but she was in a good mood, too. She said, "People know who we are now. That can't be bad."

"That's the key," said Daddy. "And Jane Slater knows who Abby is. There might be some of those horses out there who need a good rider to show what they can do."

Mom took some of the money and we went shopping—new raincoat, with a zip-out liner, so I could use it all winter, kind of an amber color with wooden buttons; two skirts, one a blue plaid and one a plain brown tweed; two long-sleeved blouses, one light blue and one white; and a Fair Isle sweater, "green heather," which would go with both the skirts. On the way home, she handed me a fifty-dollar bill, something I had never seen before. She said, "You put this in your sock drawer, and when you start going to horse shows again, you can buy yourself some tall boots. You don't have to put it in your savings account. Your dad will give you some for that. You've done a really good job."

My savings account was for the future.

I said, "Why not get the boots now?"

"Honey, you've grown three inches in the last year. No telling when that's going to stop. You don't want to outgrow them by the time you need them."

I looked at the fifty-dollar bill. It had Ulysses S. Grant on the front and the Capitol Building on the back, with some Latin writing in the seal and 50 in every corner, just so you wouldn't forget how much it was worth. It also had "Fifty Dollars" written underneath the picture of the Capitol Building. It all looked good to me, like a pair of smooth black boots that would be comfortable and easy to pull on but would go all the way up to my knees like Sophia's boots. But I didn't put the bill in my sock drawer. I folded it up and put it in an envelope and taped it to the back of a picture of Jack that was hanging above my desk.

By this time, it was almost Halloween, and Gloria decided to have a party—no trick-or-treating, just costumes and some games that her mom thought of, like bobbing for apples and pin the nose on the jack-o'-lantern. Mom helped me make a papier-mâché horse head, which I wore with Daddy's black sweater, Mom's black slacks, some papier-mâché hooves, and a tail we cut out of a piece of felt.

When we first got there, we had to enter quietly in our costumes, and the ones who were already there had to guess who was coming in. The easiest one was probably me, and the hardest one was Stella, who had tacked elastic bands to tin cans, then made the legs of her pants extra long. When she stuck her feet in the bands, it made her six inches taller than she really was, and then she wore a mask and a wig that belonged to her aunt. She made it up Gloria's walk and in the front door without falling down, and then she stood in the corner. We could not tell who she was for the longest time—until she finally laughed out loud, and we recognized her. After refreshments (pumpkin pie and chocolate ice cream), we went upstairs—the bedrooms had been made into a haunted house. The best one was in Gloria's room, where you could see through a black lace curtain that there was a corpse in the bed with open eyes and green skin (this turned out to be the kid who lived next door and went to the high school). Whenever someone came into the room, the corpse moaned. We also gave out candy to the trick-or-treaters, so it was really fun.

It was on the Monday after this party that Daddy heard from Raymond Matthews. Raymond Matthews was the son of Mr. Matthews who owned Wheatsheaf Ranch—he had gotten our number from the detective agency when he discovered that he was going to be doing business in our vicinity. Although Mr. Matthews was the owner of the ranch, Raymond Matthews was in charge of the racing division of the family businesses, and it had fallen to him to visit our place and have a look at the alleged Jaipur colt that we now had in our possession. Although he was leaving for Kentucky on Wednesday, he had set aside some time to visit us on Tuesday afternoon, if that was convenient for Daddy.

"I don't know that it is convenient," said Mom when he got off the phone.

Daddy said, "I think we have to make it convenient. I think that was the tone of his voice underneath all the polite language."

As for me, I didn't care if it was convenient or not. I

thought it would be very convenient for Jack and me to have a little walk down to the crick and to see what was going on down there. I did not think it would be at all convenient for this Raymond Matthews to see how beautiful and long-legged Jack was or to look at the cowlick in his forelock.

Daddy said, " 'Wherefore the law was our schoolmaster to bring us unto Christ, that we might be justified by faith.' Our faith is that all of this will turn out for the best." He patted me on the head, and I decided once again that I dared not pray. The rules were the rules, and they could easily go against you, if you understood them or if you didn't. So the best thing to do was just not think about it. Daddy said, "Do you understand, Ruth Abigail?"

I nodded.

Mom gave me a kiss on the cheek and squeezed my hand.

It was dark when I went out to the gelding pasture—cloudy night, no moon, chilly wind. It was November, after all, just that time of year when Pearl had been wandering around Oklahoma only a year ago. Just that time of year when Danny had moved out. I thought about myself, a year ago in seventh grade, and I seemed like such an idiot. Well, not an idiot, more like a dope. What did I know then? Not much, just to do as I was told, at home and at school. I never wondered whether doing as I was told made sense or worked out, or even why I was doing as I was told, I just did it.

I climbed onto the gate of the gelding pasture and sat on the top rail, with my heels resting on the third rail down. Lincoln and Jefferson were under one of the trees, so much in the dark that I could hardly see the difference between them. They would be good horses all their lives, and well taken care of—they didn't make trouble, they were pretty good-looking, and they weren't nervous. They always did what they were told to do, and even Mom could ride them. That was a one hundred percent good thing, until you looked at Jack.

Jack was not coming over to me because he was out in the middle of the pasture, where there was a little rise, and he was engaged in a project of his own—first he arched his neck and trotted in a semicircle, then he squealed and struck out, as if he had an enemy, then he reared up and galloped about three strides, then kicked out. Then he came back down to that snorty trot and turned the other way. It was like he was playing with an imaginary friend—a shadow on the grass or the ghost of Black George. He reared up again and walked two or three steps on his hind legs, then snorted and galloped forward. Jack was too young to do as he was told, and that was part of his beauty—who he was, how he was different from all other horses, showed up when he was not doing as he was told.

Then I saw Rusty jump the fence. She didn't jump it like a horse, she jumped it like a dog—that is, putting her forepaws on the top of the fence and pushing off—but even so, it was quite a jump, and I had never seen her do that before. Jack saw her, too, and reared up. Once she was over the fence, she crouched down for a moment, then crept toward Jack, her tail swinging slowly but silently. Jack stopped what he was doing and turned toward her, his ears pricked, his neck arched, and his tail up. At the very moment that he whinnied, she raced toward him, and I thought she was going to chase him again, the way she had that first time, but then a shape rose out of the grass and ran away, zigzagging in front of Jack for a moment,

216

then skittering to his right. Rusty was on it in a heartbeat, bringing it down and then crouching over it, shaking it. Jack reared up, wheeled, and trotted away, tossing his head.

I jumped down from the gate and walked toward Rusty, but slowly, remembering that, really, Rusty seemed like a nice dog, but we did not know her. I stopped a few steps back. She had dropped her prey. Now she walked away from it, over to me, wagging her tail. I said, "What is that, Rusty? What is that?"

It was a bobcat—I could tell by the big ears with little tufts of hair at the tips and the short tail that it wasn't one of the barn cats, though it was about the same size. It lay in the grass, its head twisted to one side, completely dead. Rusty had done a good job of that. It wasn't full-grown—a full-grown bobcat is about twice the size of a house cat and four times tougher. If she had killed one of those, there would have been more of a fight, I thought.

I looked around. Jack had moved off but was still staring at us. Right then, he put his nose to the ground and snuffled the grass for a second, then raised his head and snorted again. When I approached him, he backed up. Then I backed up, because that's what you're supposed to do when you want a horse to come toward you, but he stood where he was. I watched him for a minute, then decided that I would just leave him alone. I headed for the gate. Rusty followed me. On the porch, she went over to her blanket and curled up on it, her nose facing out.

Mom and Daddy were reading in the living room. Daddy said, "Isn't it time for you to go to bed?"

I said, "Rusty just killed a bobcat."

Both of them sat straight up. Mom said, "What?"

"Rusty just killed a bobcat in the gelding pasture. She jumped the fence and went straight for it. You should come and see."

Mom put on a sweater and we went out.

By this time, Jack was over under the trees with Lincoln and Jefferson. From the gate, you could see a dark patch in the grass, but you couldn't see what it was until you got up to it. Rusty didn't come with us. She went as far as the gate but sat down just inside the pasture and watched us. She didn't look embarrassed or worried. She looked like she knew she had done a job that needed to be done.

The dead bobcat was not in exactly the same position it had been when I left it. I said, "Jack must have moved it."

"What do you mean?" said Daddy.

"It was bent the other way. I think Jack was sniffing it while we were in the house."

Mom said, "Don't you wonder what sort of life those horses are living out here when we're minding our own business in the house?"

Daddy said, "He's an inquisitive fellow, that's for sure."

I said, "When I came out before, I thought he was just playing around, but I think the bobcat was crouched down, and he was—I don't what he was doing, but he was excited. Rearing up and snorting. Lots of things. Then Rusty jumped the fence and went for it like an arrow. At first, I thought she was going for Jack again."

"Why would she kill a bobcat?" said Mom.

"Protecting the place, probably," said Dad. "I've really never seen a dog take her responsibilities so seriously."

Mom said, "She never looks twice at the barn cats. It's

like they don't exist. I don't think she would ever chase or kill one."

The way Jack had moved the bobcat showed how young the bobcat was. The others I'd seen walking here and there on the hillsides had huge hind legs, longer than the front legs, muscular and strong. Their hair, even from a distance, looked thick and rough, nothing you would want to pet. This one was neither as tall nor as brawny as those had been. Its hair was thick, but not ratty the way it would get as the cat aged. I didn't feel much for the bobcat at the moment. Bobcats were mysterious and the opposite of friendly. When a bobcat looked at you, you never had the sense that it could ever feel anything for you.

And then there were the other things about cats, even the barn cats. One of my worst memories was coming into the barn one day when I was really young, maybe five, and two of the barn cats had a mouse between them. The mouse was running back and forth. The cats never let it get away, but they also didn't kill it. They cared about it when it moved, but when it crouched in terror, they forgot about it and licked their paws. Mom wouldn't let me watch it for long, but a few minutes was long enough—I cried myself to sleep that night and hated the barn cats for weeks afterward. Daddy just kept saying, "Cats are cats."

Well, dogs are dogs, too, and Rusty, for whatever reason, was a killer. It gave me a funny feeling, and I was sad when I went to bed.

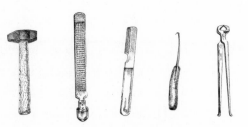

Farrier's Tools

Hoof Pick

Horseshoes

Chapter 14

Raymond Matthews showed up in a white Cadillac. I had just gotten off the school bus and was about halfway to the house when this car started honking. It took me a minute or two to realize that I was supposed to run back and get the gate for whoever was there. I opened both sides and then stood there while he drove his long white car through. He didn't wave, but he did lift one finger off the steering wheel as a thank-you. I got to the house just as Daddy was coming out to meet him, a big smile on his face. Raymond Matthews glanced at me but didn't say anything. I stood there for a second, then went inside to change my clothes. It was pretty clear that they didn't think this visit was any of my business, but I didn't agree with that. As I was heading out the door, Mom came into the kitchen, and I heard her say, "Abby—" but by that time, I was halfway to the barn.

I could see the two men by the gate to the gelding pasture. Daddy had the training halter in his hand and was just undoing the gate latch. I ran. As he was pushing open the gate, I came up to him and took the halter out of his hand, and said, "I'll do it."

I knew he wouldn't get on me with a stranger around. Raymond Matthews stepped back, like I was going to bump into him and get his suit and his shiny black shoes dirty. He was wearing a hat, too—not a Stetson, or even a straw hat, but a fancy black thing kind of down over one eye. I was sure he thought himself very handsome.

Jack and Lincoln were eating the last of the noon hay. Jefferson was chewing a board of the fence, which he stopped doing when Daddy clapped his hands at him and said, "Hey!"

Jack was friendly—he walked right over and checked my hands, thinking I might have a carrot or a bit of bread. Lincoln came after him, thinking, I was sure, that if there was something, he had first dibs. I patted Jack and slipped the rope around his neck, then I asked him to back up a half step and lower his head, which he did quite agreeably. By the time Lincoln had arrived to nudge him out of the way, I had the training halter on him. I flicked the end of the rope at Lincoln, who tossed his head as if to say, Well, who cares, anyway? He wandered back to the last of the hay. I had Jack step over a couple of times to the right and then a couple of times to the left, just to make sure he wasn't harboring any mischief. I also had him back up a step or two. He was fine. It was a warm day and he was full of hay. I turned and walked toward the gate, and Jack followed right along, not pushing ahead.

Daddy and Raymond Matthews were watching us. I wasn't sure what I wanted Jack to do. Maybe I wanted him to look weedy and small and unimpressive just so that Raymond Matthews would decide that Jack wasn't worth his time and get in his car and drive away. But I was very used to being proud of his size and strength and grace and speed, and more than that, it wasn't so much pride as love and amazement. If something was beautiful, you wanted it to keep being beautiful, no matter what. You just couldn't help yourself.

Daddy held out his hand, and I gave him the rope. He got Jack to stand up, all four feet flat on the ground and his body balanced over them. He lifted his head but wasn't extra-alert or ready to bolt—he was just himself. Raymond Matthews walked around him the way Colonel Hawkins had walked around Black George, looking at him from every angle, taking in his haunches and his legs and his shoulder and his neck and head, then doing it from the other side. That's what horsemen do—I knew all about it. You wanted every part to be right in itself and also to fit in properly with the other parts. For example, you want there to be the proper angle where the head comes into the neck, and you want the neck to taper there. If the neck doesn't taper and the angle isn't graceful, they say the horse is "hammerheaded." The bad thing about being hammerheaded is that the horse has a harder time responding to the bit he's carrying in his mouth because his neck is more inflexible. The other bad thing is that a hammerheaded horse is ugly, so beauty and grace amount to the same thing.

And then you want him to have high withers (that's the bump at the base of his neck, where the back begins), so that the saddle will sit properly on his back and not slide forward while you're riding. If you trace a line from the withers forward to the most prominent bulge on the horse's chest, you want that line to not be terribly steep, because the flatter that angle is, the more freely the front legs move. The same thing is true of the lines that run from the hip, which is where the hind leg attaches to the spine; to the point of the buttock, which is just below the base of the tail; to the stifle, which is the joint at the base of the belly; to the hock. These are a kind of spring that the horse uses to leap forward. If the angles in the spring are not too straight and not too acute, the horse moves better and lasts longer. Even the way the tail comes out of the horse's back is important, because the tail is an extension of his spine and shows how his spine is constructed.

And then there are legs. Legs are a whole subject of their own. They shouldn't turn in and they shouldn't turn out. The joints have to be big but not swollen. The bones have to be sturdy but not ugly. You don't want any swellings anywhere, and you want the hooves to be big enough to make a secure base, but not wide and flat like plates. Whole books are written about how a horse should look, and how a horse should look was how Jack looked. There was no chance that Raymond Matthews wouldn't like Jack. The thing I wanted was for Raymond Matthews to not recognize Jack.

Jack whinnied, as he often did, just to say hi, and Raymond Matthews looked at him.

He said, "No other colts to play with, huh?"

Daddy said, "We had another horse here until a few days ago who was younger than these two, and willing to play. Also, Abby here works him three times a week. He's getting plenty of activity. He works himself, really."

"Lots of get-up-and-go?" said Raymond Matthews.

Daddy nodded. I looked in the other direction.

Raymond Matthews kept walking around Jack, first one way, then the other. At one point, standing in front of him, he squatted down and stared. That was to make sure that both his knees and both his ankles and both his hooves pointed straight forward—neither knock-kneed nor bowlegged. In fact, he was just the slightest bit knock-kneed. I could see it while Raymond Matthews was looking at it. He stood up and pointed it out, then said, "But I like that in a colt. When the chest grows, the legs will turn outward. What's important is that they're symmetrical, and they are."

Oh, I thought.

"May we trot him out? Better still, can we let him run around in that pen you have? I'd like to see him move."

It was like he was buying the horse.

He said, "The mare had a distinct way of moving—very smooth and fluid. Quite often, animals in a certain line move in a similar way, and why not? Conformation and movement are very closely allied."

Daddy, Raymond Matthews, and Jack went out the gate ahead of me. It was my job to close it.

Daddy put Jack in the pen, but Jack just walked around, so Daddy said, "Abby, why don't you move him a bit for Mr. Matthews?"

I climbed over the fence with the flag in my hand. As soon as Jack saw me, and it, he flicked his tail and tossed his head. By the time I got to the center of the pen, he was trotting. I heard Mr. Matthews say, "Jaipur, of course, is a beautiful mover. Huge stride. That's why we bred the mare to him. She had no real conformation problems that had to be compensated for, and he was just a bigger, stronger version of her. Perfect match, really."

Jack was trotting around me now, his neck arched, his strides big and elegant. Who wouldn't want him?

Daddy said, "How did she do at the racetrack?"

Mr. Matthews sniffed, then said, "Oh. She had no record at the racetrack."

Daddy said, "Really? That's funny, since I saw that she had a tattoo. I never wrote it down, but I assumed that she—"

"Oh, she went to the track, but she never raced. Anything can happen at the track. She just had a little accident. But it persuaded us not to risk her value as a broodmare by pushing her."

"What was the accident?" said Daddy.

I was all ears.

Jack snorted and kicked out.

"Well, I hate to say it, but she stepped on a nail in her stall, ran it right up into the sole of the hoof and nicked the coffin bone. That kind of puncture wound can be very dangerous."

"Sure can," said Daddy.

"Took a while to get it right, and then she was always a little off, so we didn't want to risk anything. And we were right— she was an excellent broodmare. Her four-year-old won again three weeks ago. And the two-year-old is about to have his first start. The trainer is very pleased with him. He's at Churchill Downs."

Daddy said, "Shame the way those mares were treated after they were stolen."

"Yes," said Raymond Matthews. "Terrible thing."

"Especially the one mare, the chestnut with the white foot—nice name, too. What was that?"

Raymond Matthews hesitated a moment, then said, "Oh. Yes. Lucy. Lucy Lightfoot. Yes, terrible thing." I looked at Daddy. Daddy was looking at Raymond Matthews. "But the other mares and foals?"

"Oh, they're fine."

"Thank the Lord for that," said Daddy.

"Yes, indeed," said Raymond Matthews.

"How many were there again?" said Daddy.

"Four altogether, including Alabama Lady."

Daddy sniffed.

By this time, Jack was trotting around very nicely, and then he lifted into a canter. He stayed to the outside of the pen and extended his stride a little, just for fun. We were all silent as we watched him.

Daddy said, "Of course, a great-looking yearling doesn't always become a good two-year-old."

"Don't I know it! Sometimes, the ones who get to the races surprise you. Sometimes, the ones who don't get to the races surprise you."

Jack turned as easy as you please and galloped the other direction, then whinnied. Effie and Lincoln whinnied back. I stood there. I felt like I was going to cry. Here we were. Ever since the first letter came, I had been trying to not think about this very moment, this moment when I looked at Raymond Matthews and saw that he saw in Jack just what I saw—a beautiful, strong, special colt. He put his elbows on the fence and stared. Daddy's lips moved, so I knew he was praying for guidance. After a few moments, he said, "I think that's enough for the little guy."

I stepped backward and Jack turned inward, his ears pricked. He trotted two strides and then stopped in front of me and put his head down. I raised my two forefingers to either side of his head and flicked them. He backed up like he couldn't wait to do it. Raymond Matthews said, "Your daughter's done a nice job with this colt."

Daddy said, "Yes, she has. She truly has. And the colt's very fond of her." No carrot. No stick. I looked at him, but he was staring at Raymond Matthews. Then he said, "Abby, why don't you put him out now."

"Just a second," said Raymond Matthews. "Do you mind standing him up here?"

What could I do?

I stood him up. This time, Raymond Matthews touched him. He went right up to his head and put his fingers in his forelock and felt the cowlick, then he ran his fingers down either side of his mane. Then he looked at his eyes and stepped back. He said, "Thank you."

I took Jack and put him in with Lincoln and Jefferson. By that time, they were ready for their hay, so I gave them hay and the mares hay. Daddy and Raymond Matthews went into the house. I went into the house, too. They had gone into Daddy's office and closed the door. What I did was go upstairs, not to my room but to Daddy and Mom's room, which was right above the office. I closed that door. I went to the window and opened it, but I couldn't hear anything because it was cool outside and the windows downstairs were closed. I looked around for a moment, then I went over and knelt by the hot-air return vent in the corner. I could hear them perfectly.

Raymond Matthews was talking. He said, ". . . means a lot to my father and me to have found the colt after losing the mare."

"But I still don't see how you can be sure our colt is your colt."

"How could he not be? The mare you bought foaled out exactly when our mare was due. The colt looked like the mare and the sire, and has the same markings. Though the sire, of course, has a large white star—quite distinctive, actually."

"Our colt has no white markings."

"I'm looking at the cowlicks, not white marks. I realize that that makes it a bit more difficult, Mr. Lovitt, but of the brown mares sold by By Golly Sales in November of last year, one was pregnant, one gave birth, and that one came to you. She was our mare. She was stolen. We had paid the stud fee."

Now there was a long pause, and Daddy said, "How much was that?"

"Mr. Lovitt, that was seven thousand five hundred dollars."

Daddy coughed, I suppose in preference to falling out of his chair. Me, I fell over next to the heating vent and started to cry. When you expect someone to say "a thousand dollars" and they say seven times that much and more, it's quite a shock.

But I couldn't hear them talking, so I took a deep breath

and sat up again. I don't know what Daddy said when he heard that amount of money. I felt like running downstairs and looking for Mom, but I wanted to hear what would come next, so I stayed right where I was.

Daddy said, "I don't know what you're trying to pull, Mr. Matthews—"

"Me? Mr. Lovitt, we had four mares stolen. We've spent a lot of money trying to find them and have them returned. Now, I understand that you would be suspicious. That's completely as it should be. But I have my driver's license, my racing license, and Jockey Club membership document, which I've shown you. I am who I say I am, and there's no doubt who the horse is. I hate to have to repeat this to you, but the mare was the only pregnant mare at By Golly Horse Sales, and she gave birth when she was due, which was January."

He didn't sound quite as agreeable as he had.

"My daughter is very fond of the horse."

"And she's done a good job with him."

Chairs were pushed back. There was coughing and heavy breathing, and then Raymond Matthews said, "Look, Mr. Lovitt, would it be possible for me to make a phone call? Long-distance?"

"I suppose so."

Then they went out of the room.

I lay there on the floor. I could have gone to the top of the stairs and listened in on the phone call, but it wasn't easy to hide there, so I didn't. In fact, though, I didn't really want to hear the phone call. I wasn't still crying. I felt too bad for that. Then I heard Mom calling up the stairs for me, "Honey? Abby?"

So I opened the door really carefully, not making a sound, and called out, "I'm in the bathroom! Out in a minute!" Then I sat quietly in the hall until it was time to go down. As I went down the stairs, I saw Raymond Matthews talking, but I couldn't hear what he was saying, since he had his hand over the receiver.

Mom and Daddy were sitting at the kitchen table, and I guess Daddy had given Mom the news, because she looked up at me as I came into the kitchen, and she looked sad. Daddy was just staring at the table. He wouldn't look at me at all. I had to remember that they thought I didn't know what was going on, so I went over to the refrigerator and opened the door, and bent in as if I were searching for something. I straightened up with an apple in my hand when I thought I could manage to look ignorant.

But I didn't have to, because right then, Raymond Matthews came into the kitchen with a smile on his face. He said, "Well, I was lucky—I got hold of my dad and I told him about Abby here, and all you've done with the colt, and we talked about it. Sir, this is an animal with great potential, no two ways about that."

"You may say so," said Daddy. "The horse business is always chancy, as you must know."

"It is, it is." He cleared his throat. I sat down at the table, and Mom reached for my hand. Raymond Matthews went on, "Now, we fully understand that you bought the mare in good faith, Mr. Lovitt. What did you pay for her?"

"Six-fifty," said Daddy.

"And you put something into her, shipping her here and

taking care of her. So let's call your investment eleven hundred, no, twelve hundred dollars. And we owe a sort of moral penalty for not being able to hold on to our own horses." He chuckled. "So, let's take twenty-five hundred dollars off the stud fee itself. My father is willing to allow you to keep the colt, and he is a valuable colt, and we can send you the papers as soon as he is registered, for five thousand dollars. A Jaipur colt was just sold at the Keeneland July sale for twenty thousand and a filly went for sixteen thousand, which is real money for a filly. Two were sold at Saratoga this year, as well, though I don't have the prices they got at my fingertips, but—"

"I understand it's a valuable colt, Mr. Matthews. I'll have to think about it."

Mr. Matthews sat back in his chair with a smile on his face. He said, "Yes, five thousand dollars is a lot of money." He looked around the room, and you could see that he was thinking, How are these folks, with this old stove and this old refrigerator and these raggedy barn clothes hanging by the door, going to come up with five thousand dollars, enough for ten used cars or two new ones? Matthews looked at his watch. Then he said, "Of course you should think about it. I'll be here until tomorrow morning, then I'm off to England again to look at a two-year-old who's stabled at Newmarket. Nice bloodlines—half brother to Sea-Bird, who won the Epsom Derby in the spring and the Arc just a few weeks ago. Dam died, unfortunately, so this one is fairly precious."

"Lot of that going around," said Daddy.

I didn't want to know how that mare died.

"I can call you before I leave in the morning."

"Please do," said Daddy.

Everyone sat around the table for a few moments after that, the way grown-ups do, as if somehow they will start getting along if they just don't stand up right away, even though they want to. Finally, we walked him to the white Cadillac. It took him a while to turn that car around, and then he gave us one of those one-finger waves good-bye. I walked to the gate and opened it and closed it for him.

All the way back to the house, I thought how the hole in the gelding pasture would get as big as the universe once Jack was gone, at least as far as I was concerned. I went over to the gate to pat him, and he looked at me, but the geldings were busy eating their hay, so he didn't come over to the gate.

It took me a while to get into the house and hear the bad news.

Mom was making pork chops for supper, with home-fried potatoes and green beans, all things that I liked. She had them on the table by the time I opened the door (I had stopped to pet Rusty for a while before I went in, and also to straighten the row of boots on the porch, and also to wind the hose by the side of the house—I would have raked the front walk if there had been a rake). I got some dishes and started setting out the plates without her telling me. I wasn't trying to be good; I was just trying not to think about Jack getting on some van and heading off to Texas all by himself. Sure the farm was the lap of luxury, as Daddy would say. "Gold-handled faucets and silver-plated hay rakes." Other colts to play with, too— that was good. Yeah, that was good.

Mom said, "Abby, we've made up our minds about something."

I nodded.

Daddy said, "Your mom and I talked about it before, and we talked about it again just now. The colt is expensive. I have to say that I had no idea what stud fees were for horses like Jaipur. It boggles the mind."

"But," said Mom, "we have prayed about this more than once, so Mr. Matthews's visit didn't take us completely by surprise." She looked at Dad and then patted his hand, as if to say, You can do it.

And he did. He said, "Thanks to Black George, and you, we can pay what Mr. Matthews asks and keep Jack on the ranch."

What was wrong with me? I didn't even say thank you. I just sat down at the table, not able to say anything.

There was one of those silences that is really full of noise—the birds outside the window, Rusty on the porch, a horse whinnying, the house itself creaking.

Mom said, "Abby? You okay, honey?"

I said, "Oh yeah. I'm fine."

But I couldn't do it. I couldn't let Daddy give that man our money. I didn't know why. I wanted Jack more than anything in the world. I loved him, and if you'd asked me while I was standing at the gate of the gelding pasture what I wanted above all things, I would have said, "To keep Jack." But now, as Mom dished out the potatoes, I wasn't seeing Jack, I was seeing Raymond Matthews in the white Cadillac, and it seemed to me that giving him five thousand dollars was a wrong thing to do, as wrong as anything could be. And when I opened my mouth to thank them, that's what I said.

"Oh, Abby!" said Mom.

"Are you sure?" said Daddy. "Are you one hundred percent and absolutely sure?" He held up his hand. "You need to pray for guidance about this. You don't have to tell me until tomorrow morning."

But I said, "Yes, I am sure."

And I was. But I couldn't say why to save my life.

Tack Trunk

Western-Style Spurs

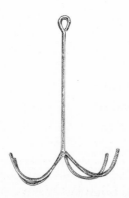

Tack Cleaning Hook

Chapter 15

I MADE IT THROUGH THE SCHOOL DAY. SOMETIMES, YOU HAVE TO make it through the school day even after your dad tells you that Raymond Matthews has said, over the phone, that a van will be at the ranch to pick up your horse the following Monday. Monday is five days away. Five days is much more than one day or two days. Five days is a pretty long time when you come to think about it. I got through the school day even though Alexis Goldman asked me if I was okay, and my algebra teacher came over and snapped his fingers right in front of me and said, "Are you with me, Abby?" and I had to say, "No," which made the other kids laugh.

Of course, if you have read *Great Expectations* and *Julius Caesar* and your class is just starting a book about three people who are lost at sea on a raft, you are supposed to understand that having a van pick up your horse the following Monday is not the worst thing that can happen to you. Assassination is worse. Being jilted at the altar and wearing your wedding dress for the next fifty years is worse. Sharks swimming around your raft is worse. But if losing your horse is the thing that is happening to you, those other things seem pretty far away.

Raymond Matthews said that the van driver would call us Friday or Saturday, that he made a regular run from Golden Gate Fields, up by San Francisco, down to Santa Anita Park. Jack would go there and then get on another van to Texas. That afternoon, I took Happy up into the hills for almost two hours. She was good. It didn't seem long enough, but it was dark when I got back. The weird thing was that I didn't work Jack. You would think that I would spend every possible moment with him, but I could hardly look at him.

The next morning, I felt different. I got up really early—before dawn—and put on my clothes and went outside. The horses were up (horses are early risers), and they nickered to me ("Hay! Hay! Don't forget the *hay*!"). So I didn't forget the hay. I also got out my chamois, and while Jack was eating from his flake and the sun was coming up, I rubbed him down until all the dust and dirt was smoothed away and his coat was shining again. He kept lifting his head from the hay and looking at me, checking my hands for carrots or bread, but he wasn't spoiled. He wasn't pushing at me or insisting, just checking as if maybe he'd missed something the last time he looked. Lincoln came over then and pinned his ears at Jack to chase him off his hay. It's a thing that horses do—they always suspect that someone else's hay is better than theirs, and they need to sample it. Jack was low on the totem pole and moved off to another pile. With three horses, you put out four piles. They might end up moving around a lot, but they all get their share. I followed Jack to his new pile and stood there with my hand on his withers.

I still didn't understand why I did what I did, but even though I was too upset to sleep in the night, I still could not stand the idea of giving Raymond Matthews five thousand dollars. I tried to think that it had to do with Jack's future. If he went back to Wheatsheaf Ranch, maybe he would go on to be a great racehorse like Jaipur, and maybe that was the best thing for him. If you had a great racehorse, how could you keep him on the ranch, working cows or going in local horse shows? If you owned Man o' War, didn't you want him to get to be Man o' War? But even though that was a nice argument, and I used it on the school bus to distract myself from Jack's actual departure (now four days away), I had made up my mind before I thought of it.

When Gloria asked me during recess (which had now turned into volleyball) what was going on, all I said was "Jack's going back to that ranch in Texas," and I walked away. Then the volleyball game began, and I didn't have to say anything more. One thing I always liked about Gloria was that if you didn't want to talk about something with her, you didn't have to.

We got through the afternoon, which included making tapioca pudding in home economics. I hated tapioca pudding.

It was when I was going to get on the school bus that I saw

Mom and our car and realized something more was happening. The thought occurred to me to just pretend I didn't see her and get on the school bus, anyway, but she smiled when she caught my eye and ran over to me. In front of all the kids, she gave me a big hug, and just as she was saying, "Oh, Abby, you won't believe—" Alexis and Barbie came over and exclaimed, "Mrs. Lovitt! How are you?"

"I'm fine, girls. How are you?"

"We're fine, too!"

Barbie said, "I hope to see you again. We had fun the last time," and held out her hand so Mom could shake it, and I thought about what a bore good manners are, but I had to smile and all of that.

In the car, Mom said, "You aren't going to believe this."

"What?"

"Guess who's at our house?"

I shrugged.

"Raymond Matthews and his father and Howard Brandt."

"He's back?"

"No."

I rolled my eyes.

Mom laughed. She said, "That person who was here Tuesday was not Raymond Matthews. He was some kind of impostor. This Raymond Matthews is completely different, kind of tall and thin."

"I don't get it."

"Abby! You were right! You were right about not trusting that Raymond Matthews! Apparently, he had forged all those things, like his racing license. He was just trying to get money from us. Somehow he heard about Jack and the story of the mare, and he was trying to swindle us."

"How did he know we had any money?"

"I don't know that."

All of a sudden, I knew something. It was like I had a rat by the tail, and I had a good grip, and all I had to do was pull it out of the hole. I pulled. I said, "Rodney Lemon."

"Who is that?"

"That's the groom out at the barn. Colonel Hawkins's groom."

"What would he have to do with it?"

"Well, he knew we had some money, because he knew all about Black George."

"But why—"

"I don't know. All I know is . . ." I pulled a little more. I could barely remember for a moment, then I did remember. I remembered Rodney Lemon standing by the gate of the gelding pasture and saying, "So that's the colt," as if he were putting two and two together. As if the colt were his business.

Mom said, "But how would Rodney Lemon know about the colt?"

"Well, I told Jane about him. That day when I went to the show and you and Daddy were at church. I was talking, and we turned into the barn aisle, and I kept talking, and he was right there, cleaning tack. I had a bad feeling, but I let it pass. I'm sure I said something about the letter, and Jane might have talked about it."

Mom shook her head. She said, "Amazing. But you were right!"

Raymond Matthews, Howard Brandt, and Warner Matthews were not driving a white Cadillac; they were driving a blue Chevrolet. It was parked by the gelding pasture, with the passenger door open. The three men were looking at the horses, and I could tell from a distance that Daddy was chatting away with them—everyone was smiling and throwing their hands around, as if they were interrupting one another. Then they all laughed. Most important, in a way, they all had cowboy hats on—not new ones, old ones, just like Daddy's. Just then, one of them saw me, then all of them turned to look. They were all smiling. But you never know what grown-ups mean when they are smiling. Lots of times they smile when they are about to tell you something for your own good.

Daddy introduced me around. Mr. Brandt was short and looked like he had never ridden a horse in his life. Raymond Matthews was about Daddy's size and shape, and Warner Matthews was old—white hair, kind of bent over, nice cowboy boots, too. He had sunglasses on, but he took them off as he said, "Well, Abby, nice to meet you," and shook my hand. His hand was dry and hard. I was sure the reason that Daddy was having such a good time with these men was that they rode horses, roped cattle, and lived on a ranch, and for the time being, it didn't matter in any way that our ranch was twenty-six acres and theirs was twenty-six thousand acres.

Daddy said, "Abby, Mr. Matthews has some good news for you."

I felt myself waking up, or something like that. Something like my hair standing on end or my skin prickling. I said, "Really?"

"Yes, ma'am," said the old Mr. Matthews. "We've been talking things over with your dad, all about the mare and this colt, Jack, and we don't feel that we can rightfully take him away from you. It still isn't absolutely certain that he's Alabama Lady's colt. Mr. Brandt here can't trace her every movement to By Golly Horse Sales—too many missing pieces. By Golly didn't happen to take any pictures of her, and neither did you, as we know."

Mr. Brandt said, "There's that other brown mare. Never did find her new owner, so there's just too many variables. Lord, I wish there was some sort of test for these animals, but there isn't."

I said, "What about the cowlick in his forelock? You said the mare had that, too."

"Oh my," said Raymond Matthews. "There's no evidence that cowlicks are inherited. You can use them to identify a horse but not to identify the offspring of that horse. Same with white marks. However the parents' white marks are arranged doesn't mean a thing for the foals."

"Just random, in my experience," said Warner Matthews.

Daddy said, "Did she ever run in races? I saw that she had a tattoo, even though I couldn't read it very well and didn't think to try and write it down."

"No, she never did," said Warner Matthews. "That trainer is very picky about running fillies. If their breeding is better than their speed, he sends them back to the ranch. Sometimes it just makes me mad, but he was right in her case. She might have done nothing as a runner, and she was a good producer from the get-go."

There was a long moment of silence while we stared at Jack, then Raymond Matthews said, "I think the lesson here is, if you got good stock, then you've got to hold on to it."

"Here's the plan," said the old man. "We are going to go to the Jockey Club and explain everything we've found to them. They are going to have to rule whether this colt is the son of Jaipur and Alabama Lady, and the likelihood is that they will decide that the doubts are too numerous for them to register him. In that case, the colt is yours, free and clear, to do with as you please."

Oh, the punch line. The Jockey Club, I thought, would be a club of jockeys. What jockey could look at him and not want to ride him? I stopped grinning. Out in the gelding pasture, Jack reared up, then galloped off, kicking all the way. All the men laughed. Raymond Matthews said, "Well, he is a lively one."

Warner Matthews said, "Yes, he is, and my private opinion is, how could he not be as well bred as we think he is? *But* you rescued the mare and you've done a wonderful job with the colt, so on the off chance that the Jockey Club rules that this is the son of Jaipur and Alabama Lady, we will own him jointly, and in another year, we can have another look at him and decide about his future. There are eighteen thousand Thoroughbreds born every year in the United States, and not many of them get to the races. I'm not going to take your horse away from you, Abby, with that kind of odds. He's thriving here. He should stay here."

Mr. Warner Matthews looked down at me and patted me on the shoulder. But I reached up and threw my arms around him, and gave him the hug of a lifetime.

The three men stayed for supper. We had fried chicken and peas and mashed potatoes, and Mom made a pumpkin pie. Raymond Matthews kept looking at Rusty, and in between supper and dessert, he got up from the table and went out on the porch. I could see them from my seat. Rusty sat square in front of him, the way she always did, with her ears up and that look on her face that made you think she was about to say something. He leaned over her and petted her once on the top of the head; then he said, "Rusty? Do you know how to roll over?" And Rusty got down and rolled over, as if she had only been waiting for someone to ask. Daddy was watching, too. He said, "That dog is beyond me."

Mom just smiled. Then she said, "It's not like I can't teach a dog a trick."

We all laughed.

It was Jane Slater who solved the mystery of the first Raymond Matthews. He was not a friend of Rodney Lemon's but a drinking buddy. Jane said, "Maybe you don't know the difference, but there is one. Remember the story I told you about Rodney and the horse knocking themselves out together? Well, there was another fellow involved in that, a man who exercises horses up at Bay Meadows, which is a racetrack south of San Francisco. Bit of a shady character. He and someone he knew concocted the plot, and the other guy was the one in the— what did you say?—white Caddy. Rodney was going on about there being a Jaipur colt from Texas in the neighborhood, and they looked up what mares had been bred two years ago to Jaipur, and there was only one from Texas. They went from there. Would Rodney have gotten a cut of the profits? He swears not, and Colonel Hawkins believes him."

I didn't know, either. I didn't blame Rodney, though maybe I would have if those men had gotten away with our money. But knowing that Rodney knew this person who knew that person who knew another person was sort of like knowing (and I did know, no matter what the Jockey Club might say) that Jack was the son of Alabama Lady and Jaipur. Right here in our pasture on our little place in our valley was a colt. When I took out my horse notebook and wrote the name of his sire next to his name, I thought of Kentucky, where Jaipur lived, and New York, where he had won famous races, and I thought of that city in India he had been named for, which I looked up in the *World Book Encyclopedia* at school. When I thought of Alabama Lady (I wrote her name just below Jaipur's), I imagined Texas and Alabama, of course, and how she must have felt wandering in the open spaces of Oklahoma. It was funny how you could imagine places you had never been. Thinking of them made you want to find out about them, look for pictures, go see them for yourself. When Raymond Matthews sent me the pedigree of the foal who was lost and maybe found, I wrote down all the names: Nasrullah, Mumtaz Begum, Rare Perfume, Eight Thirty, Sir Gallahad, Hyperion, Bull Dog, Asterus. When I closed my eyes and thought about them, they seemed to take me everywhere.

About the Author

Jane Smiley is the author of many books for adults, including *Private Life*, *Horse Heaven*, and the Pulitzer Prize–winning *A Thousand Acres*. She was inducted into the American Academy of Arts and Letters in 2001.

Jane Smiley lives in Northern California, where she rides horses every chance she gets. Her first novel for young readers, *The Georges and the Jewels*, also features Abby Lovitt and her family's ranch.